Arthur Lester Byron-Curtiss

The Life and Adventures of Nat Foster

Trapper and Hunter of the Adirondacks

Arthur Lester Byron-Curtiss

The Life and Adventures of Nat Foster
Trapper and Hunter of the Adirondacks

ISBN/EAN: 9783337180393

Printed in Europe, USA, Canada, Australia, Japan

Cover: Foto ©Raphael Reischuk / pixelio.de

More available books at **www.hansebooks.com**

THE

LIFE AND ADVENTURES

—OF—

NAT FOSTER,

TRAPPER AND HUNTER OF THE ADIRONDACKS,

—BY—

A. L. BYRON-CURTISS.

UTICA, N. Y.:
Press of Thomas J. Griffiths, 131 Genesee Street.
1897.

PREFACE.

In writing this book, I have not catered to the novel reader or sensational book worm. A "plot" could have been introduced, and, weaving it into the fabric of the whole, the work could have been easily changed from the historical to the romantic, and a good novel made; so I have been told by a few of my friends, who have done me the kindness to examine the MSS., or have submitted to the ordeal of having some of it read to them. But it is in no sense a work of fiction. It is a faithful account of the life and adventures of a character familiar to sportsmen and others who frequent the Adirondacks. It has been my endeavor to collect and put in form the numerous stories and anecdotes told by one of the pioneers of New York State; though in my desire to vindicate the qualities of Nat Foster, I have given considerable not actually identified with his adventures, but having a bearing on his life.

The hardy race of men who followed the chase for a livelihood in the wilds of Northern New York, has passed away. With the men has gone the knowledge of many of their exciting adventures. It is not too late, however, to gather

from old residents and descendants, many of
the experiences connected with their profes-
sion. This is what I have endeavored to do in
this book; taking pains, as the reader will see,
to gather only such notes of Foster's life as the
trustworthy sources assured me of their
genuineness. The assumption that Foster is
the hero of Cooper's Leatherstocking Tales I
think is well founded. I believe the reader
will agree with me, that the character of Nat
Foster as portrayed by the facts here presented, and the character of Natty Bumfo of
Cooper, are wonderfully similar; which, taken
with the unbiased opinions of men of Foster's
time, are weighty arguments in favor of the idea
advanced. I am sure my labors will be appre-
ciated by those interested. And as Jerome K.
Jerome observed in his "Idle Thoughts of an
Idle Fellow," that "some of my relations having
promised to buy the book, if it ever came out;"
so I would say that many persons interested in
the Adirondacks, having expressed a desire to
own the book "if it ever came out." I feel justi-
fied in inflicting it on the public. I would in
conclusion express my thanks to those who
have in any way contributed to the material
that makes up the book.

Rome, N. Y., April, 1897. *The Author.*

CONTENTS.

CHAPTER V.

CHAPTER VI.

CHAPTER VII.

CHAPTER VIII.

CHAPTER IX.

CHAPTER X.

ILLUSTRATIONS.

—

CHAPTER I.

NATHANIEL Foster, the hero of this book, was of New England stock. His father, whose name was Nathaniel, was born in Rhode Island, and some time after the close of the French and Indian war, married, and with his young wife, emigrated to Hinsdale, New Hampshire. At the time of his settlement at Hinsdale, it was in the strictest sense a pioneer town, situated near the mouth of the Ashuelat River, and hard by the Connecticut.

Its territory, except the few acres cleared by the settlers, was covered by virgin forests. Almost all the inhabitants lived in the most primitive manner possible to civilized people. Log houses on squatters' farms formed the bulk of the little hamlet. A few sheep and cows, a yoke of oxen, and possibly a horse, was owned by those settlers who had been a few years at the place. Upon a few acres of land cleared by earnest toil, was raised Indian corn and Irish potatoes. These formed the staple articles of their vegetable diet. The woods, abounding with game, supplied them with meat.

Mr. Foster, having selected a favorable site for his new house some two miles from the settlement proper, proceeded first to erect his log house, and then attacked the forest. In a couple of years he had a number of acres cleared, and under cultivation. The second year of his settlement, the birth of a son gladdened the hearts of the young couple. Elisha, the oldest of the family, and next to Nathaniel, being born in 1764.

Moose and deer were plentiful, while the gray wolf and the panther made the nights hideous by their howls and screams. Black bears were numerous. Mr. Foster, being a crack shot, kept his larder well supplied with wild meats, while the pelts of the fur-bearing animals took the place of ordinary bedding and blankets. For being tanned with the hair on they furnished warm robes for protection from the icy cold of the New England winters. The meat of the deer, moose and black bear was corned, smoked, and dried. A great deal of the wild game of the woods was of course a source of annoyance to the settlers, in their attempts to raise domestic animals. Often after a settler had, by several seasons' patient breeding, obtained quite a flock of sheep, or a number of cows; or from one sow had obtained a promising litter of shoats, his plans and calculations were upset by some nocturnal visitor from the woods. gaining access to the sheep fold or pigsty, and slaughtering one or more of the animals, before the owner could become aware of what was going on, and rising from his bed, go forth, gun in hand, to drive the intruder away.

Even in the daytime some wild animals attacked the domestic ones, if they wandered far into the woods. The pigs were never permitted to go into the woods in the fall to root for acorns, without being accompanied by a man with a gun, to shoot any bear which might wish to change its diet from wild berries to fresh pork.

The New England Colonies early began offering bounties for the slaughter of these wild animals, and the pine-tree shilling was a welcome reward to the struggling frontiersmen, in their contest with the wild beasts of the wilderness they were trying to subdue.

The wild animals were not so great a source of danger to the settlers' flocks of domestic ones, however, as the Indians, the latter really being their greatest enemies in this respect. There were still roving bands of these aborigines, not yet inclined to succumb to the advancements of the pale-face. These would ap-

proach the settlements to steal, sometimes even
bold enough at that late day, to sack and burn
the dwellings, and murder and scalp the inmates. Just before the outbreak of the war of
the Revolution, a small hamlet a few miles from
Hinsdale was destroyed in this way.

As the colonial spirit of independence increased, these depredations on the part of the
Indians grew more frequent and bold. But one
noticeable feature connected with all Indian
raids was, that it was always the patriot families
whose stock was stolen, while the Tories' property would remain undisturbed; so that they
were soon suspected of exciting the Indians to
their nefarious business by gifts of rum and
tobacco.

Conspicuous among the Tory families at
Hinsdale at this time was one by the name of
Wilson. William Wilson was a prominent man
in the village, which by this time had gotten to
be quite a town. He held a lucrative position
for those days, under the service of the Crown,
and was the stamp-agent under the famous
Stamp Act. Hence he was a marked loyalist.
He lived very comfortably in the only frame
dwelling in the hamlet, kept a couple of servants, and sent his only child, a daughter, to
school in Boston. He had a great many doings

with the Indians under the guise of a trader, and was thoroughly suspected by the patriots of being one of the chief ones who encouraged the Indians in plundering and stealing from the patriotic settlers on the frontier. So numerous and bold had the Indians become, that Mr. Foster, in less than a year, had all of his cows stolen, and a flock of thirty sheep reduced to six. One day, during his absence from home, their only remaining pig, a sow, was stolen.

Upon his discovery and report of the loss, his Tory neighbors offered as explanation that a wild animal had taken it; but he scouted this idea, and declared that it was mighty funny that a panther or wolf would steal a pig from its sty in broad daylight. "No," said he, "it was none of your four legged varmits that done it. I reckon it was them two legged ones you're a settin' on us."

The suffering patriots could not shoot their Tory neghbors, but it is needless to say that they dealt with the Indians in the same manner as they dealt with wild animals that stole from their flocks. They shot them.

Under such circumstances, and at such times as these, was Nathaniel Foster, Jr., born, on the 30th day of June, 1766, nine years prior to the outbreak of the war for Independence. And

as we read of the hardy days of his boyhood, and
the struggle of his family for existence, intensified by the depredations of Indians, his own
young life environed by influences of the woods,
we do not wonder at his remarkable career as
a hunter and trapper, and the hardiness he displayed in following that pursuit. Nor can we
wonder at the indifference he sometimes displayed in making away with such Indians as
were unfortunate enough to imagine that they
could cross him in the following of his chosen
calling in the Adirondack Mountains.

The elder Nathaniel, being an ardent patriot,
was a leader in holding meetings in the township, in the interest of liberty. When Nathaniel,
Jr., was scarcely seven years old, he and his
brother Elisha asked their father to take them
to one of these meetings. At first he demurred, but finally yielded to their importuni-
ties, and took them along with him; with considerable grumbling, however, saying they
would only be "under foot and in his way." At
this meeting, Mr. Foster made a rousing
speech, following the popular and usual strain
of the time of "give me liberty, or give me
death." In closing he exclaimed impressively,
"I am ready now to go and fight the Crown."
Young Nat, who with his brother occupied a

"Nat *** with his brother occupied a back seat."

back seat, had listened with open mouth (and ears) to his father's flow of patriotic and revolutionary expressions, and seemed to have caught the spirit of the occasion; for as his father uttered the above words, he piped up from his seat in the corner, in a shrill but defiant little voice, "Yes, dad, you go, and Lish and me'll stay home and shoot Injuns." This childish expression of patriotism and defiance of the Crown was greeted with exclamations of delight from the hardy pioneers present. Nat was brought from his seat in the corner, greeted with three hearty cheers from their lusty lungs, and the meeting dispersed.

Less than two years passed ere his father did go to "fight the Crown," and Elisha and Nat were left at home to "shoot Injuns." But not to shoot Indians only; but also to participate in, and share the hardships and privations which the patriotic families of those times were called upon to endure, while the heads of the families were away "fighting the Crown," and gaining for us that priceless heritage of liberty, which we all enjoy, but do not appreciate one half or one quarter as much as we should.

CHAPTER II.

EARLY in 1775, Mr. Foster began to make preparations for going to war. The idea that war might possibly be averted seemed never to have been entertained by him. The words of Patrick Henry had so enthused the people throughout the land, that the men would swing their hats and exclaim, "Give me liberty or give me death." On the first day of February Mr. Foster gathered his family about him, and gave each an affectionate farewell, and blessing; for he was a pious man. He then shouldered his musket and started on foot for Boston. The family then consisted of Mrs. Foster and six vigorous, growing children. Elisha, the oldest, was eleven years old; Nathaniel, our hero, was nine; Zilpha, a girl of seven summers; destined in after years to play the most conspicuous part in an exciting adventure. The next youngest child was a daughter Ann, aged five. The next, a boy of three, bearing the ponderous name of Solomon; the youngest child was a cooing babe named Sylby, scarcely a year old. Mrs. Foster and these six children did not see

Mr. Foster again until the close of the war, over seven years and ten months after he took his departure on that frosty February morning.

All their earthly possessions at this time consisted of some ten acres of cleared land, one cow, a few sheep, two pigs, and a few fowls. And their struggle with poverty and actual want during the absence of the husband and father, was truly a gallant one. But let us leave them for a little, and follow the fortunes and experiences of the head of the family. The elder Foster's career in the war has such an important and indisputable bearing and relation to the subsequent career of his family, particularly that of his son Nat, that we will devote this and the next two chapters to an account of some of his adventures and experiences in the war. Journeying on foot he reached Concord the last of the month. As he plainly saw, the war was soon to break out; so he remained in the vicinity, exhorting and encouraging the minute men in their preparations for taking the field. In a couple of months after his arrival in Concord, he had the satisfaction of participating in the battle of Lexington, and firing his first shot at the Crown, as represented in the British troops that invaded Concord. He was in the thickest of the fight, and with other patriots,

poured his deadly fire from behind stone fences
and trees, into the ranks of the royal troops as
they retreated towards Boston. He received
two bullet holes in his clothes, and exultingly
exclaimed as he discovered them, "I'll be able
to fight a good many years if the red-coats only
shoot cloth."

He immediately repaired to Boston, and
presenting himself to Col. Prescott, was assigned by that officer to a prominent place
among the patriot troops then throwing up in-
trenchments on Bunker Hill. His bravery,
skill and enthusiasm at this battle, made him
ever afterwards a favorite with the officers and
men of the American Army who knew or heard
of his conduct on the heights of Boston. He
did much by his own coolness and presence of
mind to further the efforts of Col. Prescott,
who, it will be remembered, preserved order,
and kept up the courage of the raw American
soldiers by his own calmness and courage.
When the ammunition gave out, and the British
commenced to pour over the breast-works,
Foster was the first to club his gun, and shouting "Give it to them, boys," commenced to club
the red coated soldiers right and left. As we
know, all the soldiers "clubbed" their muskets,
and endeavored to resist effectually the on-

coming British; but it was a hopeless task. Foster and the few remaining with him fled down a desperately steep place on the hill, and thus escaped through the dust and smoke of the battle. Foster was promptly offered a captain's commission in the Continental Army, as a reward for his conspicuously gallant conduct at this battle; but he declined the honor and responsibility.

Washington having been appointed in charge of the army of the East, commenced to fortify the heights around Boston, and Gen. Howe moved the Royal troops in the vicinity to a greater distance from the toiling Yankees. His treatment at their hands at Bunker Hill seemed to have taught him a lesson, so that he now appeared to have some little respect for the despised American pioneers. This movement on the part of the enemy was of course a subject of conversation among the American soldiers, and Foster in one of his characteristic expressions said, "Let 'em go: Let 'em go to Halifax," a settlement in Canada. This expression was taken up by the rest of the soldiers. It passed from mouth to mouth. Washington laughed as he heard of the apt way it was expressed. It soon became a by-word in the army, and is now common property, "Go to Halifax."

Foster seems to have been in the army under Gen. Putnam. At all events, he accompanied the American army to New York, and, at the head of forty picked men, harassed the Britons from behind the rocks at Harlem Heights, effectually protecting Washington's retreat to White Plains. Several of the enemies' bullets passed through his clothing again; and one grazed his left side, cutting the skin so that it bled profusely, and he was obliged to go to a surgeon. That officer put on his spectacles, and gravely examining it, remarked, "My good man, if it had gone a little closer it would have killed you." "Yes, yes," said Foster, in his indifferent manner, "and if it had only gone a little farther off it wouldn't have touched me." During Washington's retreat through New Jersey, Foster was one of his trusted men. For his enthusiasm, endurance and courage, he had no superior. Washington remarked that the enthusiasm and devotion to the cause, of such men as Foster, gave him courage to continue the struggle against such great odds. And on one occasion he was heard to say that with ten thousand such men as Foster he could drive every British soldier from the American shores in short order. Foster was one of the picked men who preceded the army to the Delaware River, and got boats in readiness to pass over. On the 23rd of December, 1776, Washington was seen on his knees asking divine aid and guidance for the then almost hopeless cause of his country. On the same day he called a council of officers to consider the feasibility of attacking the Hessians encamped at Trenton. But few advised it, when Foster came forward, and offered the efficient aid of his "picked forty," and it was decided to undertake it. Foster returned to his companions, and telling them of the acceptance of their services, exclaimed, "Boys we'll have a Christmas dinner off from Trenton, or die in the attempt to get it." History tells us of Col. Rohl's surrender, the capture of a thousand Hessians, and the safe retreat of Washington and his army across the Delaware again. The battle of Trenton and its results roused the colonies from despondency. Foster, for his bravery and efficient services on this occasion was again offered a captain's commission. But he again declined the honor, and this time in words which effectually prevented the office being tendered him again; he said to the orderly who brought the message to him, "No, I came to fight the common enemy of our country, and I can do that better with a gun than with a sword; I'll stick to my gun."

The following spring he was ordered with his "picked forty" up the Hudson to assist Gen. Gates. To him they rendered good service at the battle of Saratoga. Occupying a brow of a hill, they contributed materially to the success of the battle by their rapid and accurate firing. As the royal army retreated they were able from their position to pour a destructive fire into the ranks of the enemy. Every shot counted. Foster's exhortation to his men as they took their position on the hill was, "Now boys, don't waste a shot. Bring down a red coat every time you fire." We all know the results of that battle. Gen. Burgoyne surrendered, and the Americans marched into his camp to the tune of "Yankee Doodle." It was at this battle that Arnold won laurels he ought to have worn; and if he had, his subsequent act of treason might not have occurred.

Before participating in the battle of Saratoga, however, Foster and his forty "dare devils," as they had come to be called, took a journey up the Mohawk Valley. They participated in the battle of Oriskany, having joined Gen. Herkimer's minute men at Fort Dayton. They then started leisurely back to Saratoga, when they met the detachment headed by Arnold sent for the relief of Fort Stanwix. They joined them,

"Their ascent of a slight eminence."

and returned back over the ground they had twice gone over, past the bloody field of Oriskany, and on to Fort Stanwix. Then they started on down the valley again. It appears that they traveled by themselves rather than with the regular troops. It was during his journeys up and down the Mohawk Valley at this time, that Foster saw so much of the diabolical acts of the Indians in slaying and scalping the defenseless settlers, at the instigation of the British, and which caused him on his return home, to instill into the minds of his sons such a hatred of the race.

While he and his party were returning down the valley from Fort Stanwix, as they came where Canajoharie now stands, then almost a wilderness, their ascent of a slight eminence brought to their view on the north an immense smoke rising from the tree-tops. Said Foster, "I guess some of the red devils are putting in their hellish work." Sure enough, as they proceeded, they came in sight of a log cabin in flames, and an immense crowd of Indians around it. The little band of forty immediately prepared for a rush upon them. They crept cautiously forward under the cover of trees and bushes, until they could see plainly some two score of savages dancing about the cabin. They knew by their actions that there were people in the dwelling, and they were waiting for them to come out from the blazing building, when they intended to set upon them, and slay and scalp them.

"Attend to your priming, boys," said Foster, "We'll show the red cusses that the Yankees arn't all napping." He gave the word to fire, and instantly twelve Indians lay upon the ground in their death throes, and several were wounded. The Indians, though taken by surprise, rallied for resistance, and made for trees, from behind which they always fired. But before half a dozen of them could reach the shelter of tree trunks, Foster's men fired another volley into them. It was effectual. All signs of a resistance disappeared with the Indians' disappearance in the woods. The brave little band of soldiers now rushed forward to the house, which was burning furiously. The door and windows they found barricaded. It was but the work of a moment to smash in the door with a small log which lay handy, and the inmates were dragged from the doomed cabin none too soon. They were a Mrs. Failing and her three small children. They had all been overcome by the smoke and heat, and were insensible when removed from the burning house, the mother having been quite badly burned. Water brought from a neighboring spring in the hats of some of the men, and dashed in their faces, soon brought them to their senses. When they realized deliverance, their gratitude was beyond expression. The husband and father of the family was away fighting for liberty. Had this little band of patriots been but a few moments later in their arrival on the scene, his family would have been burned alive. The mother and children were taken to the nearest settlement, and placed among friends; Foster and his party remaining there for several days, fearing that the Indians might seek revenge by attacking the settlement. Word finally being brought them that a battle was likely to be fought very soon at Saratoga, they took leave of the settlement and the family they had saved, and pushing on, joined the American army, rendering the efficient service from their position on the hill, as mentioned above.

After Burgoyne's surrender it was feared that an attack would be made by the large number of Indians that the British had assembled, and a force of soldiers most familiar with the Indian mode of warfare, was dispatched in the direction of Lake George, to disperse a horde of the savages reported to be there. Foster and his forty were chosen, together with about thirty regular soldiers. Towards nightfall they surprised and dispersed a camp of about seventy-five Indians, as they were engaged in cooking their supper. The encounter was not at all a serious one, for the Indians at the approach of the detachment, stopped only to let drive a shower of bullets and arrows; and then turned and fled, leaving in the camp a quantity of guns, bows and arrows. As their fires were burning, the soldiers tarried at the camp long enough to cook rations for themselves, and rest a little before returning to the army. Foster and his men quickly made the acquaintance of their new companions who had been detailed to accompany them on the scout; and while seated around a fire eating their food, he gave their new friends some account of the experience of himself and his men up the valley. He related one after another of their adventures until he came to the incident of the burning house, and the rescue of the inmates. As he proceeded with the narration, one of the soldiers seated on a log opposite Foster, sprang to his feet, and seizing Foster in his arms, commenced to weep like a child. "That was my home, and those were my children," said he, "how can I ever pay you for such a humane act?" "Pay me," said

Foster, "I would be worse than a heathen if I would not risk my own life, to save the lives of a man's wife and children from such a fate. But hold," he exclaimed, as Failing, who had regained his composure, was about to resume his seat on the log, "hold," repeated Foster, "Swear to me, swear, that you will kill every red devil you get a chance to." And with bared head and uplifted hand, Failing swore to prosecute a war of extermination against the red man.

Foster now became very excited, and vehemently declared his hatred of the race. Addressing the group of men before him he exclaimed, "Boys, I've seen enough of their fiendishness in our excursions up the valley, to make me and my children forever their enemies." He then related how he had seen the soldiers scalped at Oriskany. How in one place they had come to a devasted home, with the women and children strewn about scalped and bearing witness to the use of the tomahawk. The worst and most repulsive sight of all was the body of a pregnant woman ripped open, and the infant mutilated. "That is what I've seen," said he, "during the last few weeks, and can a man with a Christian heart allow such hounds of hell to go unpunished? No! The sight of

a red skin kindles a fire in me I can't control,
and which I don't want to either." In such a
strain he continued talking for some time. His
expressions of hatred of the British for exciting
the Indians to hostility, was nearly as pronounced. Said he, "They are more to be despised than the Indians themselves. We'll lick
the British, and then we can fight the Injuns,
and when we are dead, our children will do the
fighting for us." He declared he would teach
his children to fear God, but not the face of clay.
"Especially," he said, "the copper face of an
Injun." Again can we see the reason his son
Nat placed a low value on the life of any member of this unfortunate race with whom he came
in contact, while threading his way among the
forests of the Adirondacks.

CHAPTER III.

THE American army now went into winter quarters at Valley Forge, where the patriots bravely endured untold sufferings. It has been said of this particular winter that "These were the times which tried men's souls." The Patriot army was a mere handful of men compared to the British. The men were ragged and disheartened; many were barefooted. What American of the present generation is there, who has not seen from childhood illustrations of the pathetic scenes of Valley Forge? The members of the army had received no pay, and poor and scanty fare was their portion. The soldiers were inspired by a love for their country indeed.

During this trying winter, Mr. Foster was the life and soul of his section of the camp. He was never idle or despondent. No doubt his being always busy at some kind of employment, was the secret of his cheerfulness. He was always ready for a joke or a word of cheer. The horses of the army were being killed for food. He immediately set about and procured the hides for the purpose of making shoes for the soldiers. He tanned them in a rude manner; and with the assistance of some of his fellow-soldiers, he made a passable moccasin, very acceptable to the barefooted men. It was while engaged in this occupation of cutting up hides and making shoes, that Washington, passing through the camp one day, and observing his industry and cheerful manner, uttered the remark referred to before; viz.: "If I had ten thousand such men, I would drive every British soldier from the American shores in short order." One day provisions failed to be issued at all. Some stores had been expected, but were delayed many miles distant, the wagons being stuck fast in the mud. The soldiers were disposed to grumble and swear at the state of affairs.

"Well, well boys," exclaimed the ever-cheerful Foster, "we musn't starve, and we shan't. Hunger will drive a man through a stone wall, but we are not as bad off as that yet. I've got some scraps of horse hide left over from making shoes, and I guess it will make a soup for about ten or a dozen." The soup was made, and with a little "johnny cake" left over from the day before, Foster and his mess ate it with a relish.

"There boys, said he, as the meal was finished, "that's pleasanter than marching twenty-
five miles over a frozen road, especially if you've
got a sore toe, to kick the frozen lumps with."

This memorable winter, full of trials and
sufferings, finally passed away; and preparations
were begun for an active campaign. After the
battle of Monmouth, the army was busy preparing for the capture of Stony Point. Hearing
of the massacre at Wyoming Valley, a detachment of four hundred men were sent to the
scene. Foster and his "forty," now reduced to
less than thirty, were among the first to arrive.
The sight they saw of slaughtered men and
mutilated women, before they reached the fort,
sickened them. But what they saw when they
got to the fort, destroyed their feelings of qualm-
ishness, and roused their indignation and
wrath. The fort had been the refuge for the
inhabitants of the valley: and thus crowded with
human beings it had been fired by the savage
foe. The fire, though not destroying the
stockade, had brought death to women and
children. The soldiers of the garrison, aided by
the men from among the refugees, had evidently fought both the fire and the enemy to the
very last man. Dead men, shot, scalped, and
tomahawked, were found everywhere, both out-

side and inside the fort, but not one was alive to tell of the gallant resistance they must have made.

But the most awful sight of all, was the charred bodies of the women and children, lying in a heap of ashes and smoldering timbers in the center of the fort. They had evidently taken refuge in the soldiers' barracks; and as the men were shot down and killed, were left defenceless to be literally roasted alive. The bodies lay heaped together like so many logs, and were burned beyond recognition. Mr. Foster never forgot this scene. Ever afterwards, even in his old age, if he referred to it, it was with bitter, wrathy and denunciatory language.

The winter quarters of 1779-80 were at Morristown, N. J. The soldiers fared better than at Valley Forge, as they were better clothed, but provisions were scarce. A pint of corn was often the daily allowance per man; each mess put this together, and pounding it up in a stone mortar, they made a passable johnny cake. Occasionally a little meat would be issued, more often than not the flesh of the horse. Towards spring potatoes were issued, being procured from the interior. These baked in hot ashes were a welcome addition to the bill of fare. It was during one of Mr. Foster's excursions to the northern part of New Jersey in search of supplies at this time, that he captured a horse which afterwards played an important part in connection with the pretended desertion of Sergeant John Champ, in an attempt to carry out the plans of Washington and Lee for the capture of Arnold, after his treason. In one of their journeys in search of food, Foster and his men made their way to the home of an old Tory named Piser. This man was known to smuggle provisions through the country to the Loyalists in New York City and Philadelphia, where they were sold to the British. Foster had heard of this man, and so this day, pushed on up the State until he arrived at his house. Leaving his companions in the yard, he boldly went to the front door of the spacious mansion, and demanded of the old darky who answered his knock, to see the master.

"Deed sah," said the darky, eyeing the unkempt and ragged patriot before him, "I reckon he don't see such as you."

"He don't eh?" answered Foster, "Well, you tell him to see me or I'll see him, and mighty quick, too."

Piser having heard the parley at the door, now came forward and mildly asked Foster what he wanted.

"To buy some provisions for the Continental army," was Foster's brief answer.

"I haven't any provisions," answered Piser, "and besides," he continued, falling into the whining tone characteristic of miserly men, "If I had any you couldn't pay me for them."

"Couldn't pay you for 'em," said Foster, "I'll give you Continental money for 'em, and any patriot will take that.

But still Piser asserted that he had no stores about his place.

"Now see here," said Foster, growing impatient, "you've got plenty of provisions on hand, and you know it. And if you don't trot 'em out, me and my men 'll take 'em away." But still he declared he had none.

"You can look and see, you can look and see, but you will find nothing," said the old Tory.

"Yes, we'll look and see, and we'll find some, too," answered Foster, confidently.

He returned to his waiting companions and they began a search of the barns, smoke house, and other out-buildings. But as Piser had told them, they found nothing. But there was an old block house a short distance from the other buildings, which had not been searched. It stood on a slight elevation of ground, and apparently was unused. After giving up the search in the barns, Foster proposed investigating this building. At this Piser, who had followed them about the place, assured them, in the most courteous tones, and voluminous language, that that was wholly unnecessary. The block house, he told them, had been built in the days when attacks from Indians were frequent, but had been unused for a number of years. There was nothing in it, he assured them. It was empty and locked. In fact, he told them, it had been padlocked so many years that the fastenings had become rusted, and only the other day he had tried the key to it but it would not work, and he had let it go.

"Oh, I assure you, sir," said he, addressing Foster, "there is not the slightest necessity of searching the block house."

"Oh, no, I don't suppose there is a bit o' use," said Foster, at the same time slyly winking to his companions. "Howsoever we might just as well, though;" he added, "I'd kinder like to see how the old thing looks inside."

Accordingly he led the way to the old weather beaten building and without troubling the owner for the key to the lock, which did not look so very rusty after all, they broke open the door with the butts of their muskets, when lo and behold, they found it filled with stores. There

were eight dressed hogs, evidently ready for
shipment; and a large quantity of corn and
potatoes already sacked, also ready for shipment. And in one corner, safely stalled, was an
elegant black horse as the men had ever seen.
The old Tory had prepared to convey the provisions to the river that very night, and with the
cargo he was intending to send the black
charger to Gen. Clinton of the British army.

Further parley was unnecessary. The men
returned to the barns in search of something in
which to carry some of the stores away with
them. They found two old carts, such as were
then in use on many of the old colonial farms;
the two wheels made from solid sections of wood
sawed from a log, were placed at the center of
a spacious box. The axle was hard maple. A
rough pole or tongue made of a limb of a tree,
extended from the forward end of the box to
which the oxen were yoked. Although rude,
these carts were very serviceable, and with patient but sure pulling oxen, large loads could be
drawn on them. There was but one pair of
oxen about the place. These the men yoked
and hitched to one cart, and trailing the other
behind, returned to the block house where they
loaded both with as much of the corn and potatoes as could be piled on. Then placing four

"The old Tory was wild with rage."

pigs on each load, "just to bind the loads," as Foster explained to Piser, they were prepared to return to camp.

The old Tory was wild with rage as he saw them removing his stuff and preparing to make off with it. He cursed them and the whole Continental army, from Washington down. He cursed the spirit of independence which brought on the war, and he cursed those who were fighting to gain that independence.

After Foster had stood it long enough he told the old man to "shut up," or he would make short work of him. And when a half a dozen of his comrades cocked their guns and pointed them at him, the warning was apparently too realistic, and he held his tongue, and remained as quiet as a lamb. When they were ready to start, Foster turned to Piser and asked him if he would take Continental currency for his stuff.

"No," shouted Piser, his rage bursting out again, "I'll take none of your d——d currency; it's no better than your d——d government, which will be out of existence in a short time."

"I reckon you'd think different if the light was a shinin' through your old carcass," said Foster. You're so pizenly mean I orter make it shine through ye right now. It would sarve you right. But seein' you're so mighty pat-

riotic," he continued, assuming a sarcastic air,
"I guess I'll let you go and take that black hoss
instead." "Jedediah," said he, addressing one
of his party, "bring out the hoss." The noble
steed was led out, amid the frantic protests of
Piser, who swore vengeance upon them for this
last act of taking the valuable horse. But no
attention was paid to him. Putting their shoulders to the trailing cart and speaking a "gee up"
to the oxen they were off.

It was the last they ever saw of the old Tory.
He watched them go, driving his sleek oxen and
leading his magnificent horse, bearing with
them provisions that were to bring a square
meal to many a hungry soldier fighting for the
cause of Freedom. But no such thoughts filled
his mind. Only the loss of his property and the
disappointment of not receiving a few pounds
of English money for it, was what occupied his
small soul. Cursing and shaking his fist at them
until they were out of sight, he returned to his
house to brood over his ill luck, and growl at
the spirit of liberty and freedom God had planted in the hearts of his fellow man, if not in his.

The arrival in camp of Foster and his men
with such a bountiful supply of provisions, was
hailed with delight. Although it was dark, fires
were started, or those already burning made to

blaze brightly. Potatoes were distributed, and a couple of the hogs cut up at once and passed around. All went to sleep that night with a full stomach, and a taste of fresh pork in their mouths.

The handsome horse Foster brought into camp was at once a center of attraction. He was led up to one of the fires and examined and admired. Foster explained and pointed out his good points. He declared that it was the soundest, fleetest, easiest riding and most gentle "hoss" ever raised in the Colonies. How he had discovered all this during the short time the horse had been in his possession, would be hard to explain. But it is to be presumed that he felt obliged to impress upon his fellow soldiers the superiority of this particular horse which he had captured from a detestable old Tory.

"Why, boys," said he, addressing a fresh group of admirers, "its jest like riding in a rocking chair, a riding him bareback; what must it be when he has got a saddle on?" When asked what he was going to do with the horse, he said, "Why give him to the major, of course," meaning Major Lee. So, after he had himself partaken of a hearty meal of potatoes and pork, the former baked in hot ashes, and the latter toasted at the end of a ramrod, he made his way to the major's tent. Presenting himself to that officer, he told him in a brief manner of the day's experiences, and ended by telling Maj. Lee that he had brought the horse expressly for him. Without waiting for thanks he turned to go, when the major stopped him and said:

"My good man, don't you want to join the Legion?"—a body of men immediately connected with Major Lee.

"I'll do anything that will serve my country to the best advantage," was Foster's simple reply.

"Then you are just the man I want," answered Major Lee, quickly, struck with the answer Foster gave. "You may come to my tent to-morrow night at eight o'clock and bring the horse with you," and added, "he may be of great service to us at once."

Foster made respectful answer, replying that he would be on hand at the appointed hour, and withdrew. The next night at the hour appointed by Major Lee, Foster repaired to the major's tent, leading his black horse. He had carefully groomed the animal, and had procured an old bridle and saddle for it; for he felt sure that Major Lee was going to assign him a duty which would demand his own use of the horse that night. Such proved to be the case.

Arriving at officers' headquarters, he tied the horse to a sapling, and approached the sentinel. As the guard challenged him, a tall man with his face concealed by a cloak wrapped about his shoulders, spoke to the sentry, and Foster was allowed to pass. The stranger then beckoning to Foster, led the way into the officer's tent, where he threw off his cloak and revealed himself in the garb of a common soldier with sergeant's chevrons on his sleeves. The two men gazed at each other in mutual admiration. Both were types of perfect men, six feet tall and straight as arrows. It was the first meeting of Foster and Sergeant John Champ, though each had heard of the deeds of bravery and daring, and of the valor, of the other. Major Lee, at this moment, entered the apartment, and saluting him, the two stalwart patriots were seated. Major Lee then made known the plans of himself and Washington for the capture of Arnold, the traitor. We are all familiar with the details of Arnold's treason, who, to satisfy his feelings of revenge for not receiving proper rewards for his brave service at the battle of Saratoga, would have betrayed his country for a few thousand pounds of English money. Verbose and complete accounts of it are found in the various histories of the United States,

4

though, as usual, little justice is done to the fallen one, or for that matter, to any of the unsuccessful intriguers connected with the despicable plot. But it is not my place now to discuss the character or motives of Arnold, but to follow the adventures of the father of Nat Foster, in connection with the plans of Washington and Lee, for the capture of the traitor; and as I have not seen any detailed accounts of them in any of the histories of the United States, I will give them as they were told to me by a great-grandson of the elder Foster. The plans were to have a trusted soldier desert to the British, and going to New York City, there lay plans for the capture of Arnold and his return to the American lines. Sergeant John Champ was the man selected for this hazardous task; and it was to arrange for the initial step that the conference was now being held in Major Lee's tent. Champ had been previously made aware of the desperate work assigned to him, but Foster was still ignorant of any of it.

Seating himself, Major Lee addressed both of the men before him thus: "My brave men, you have an important duty to perform. The plans of Washington and myself must be carried out, if possible. Since the treason of Arnold we hardly know whom to trust, either among the

officers or the men, but I feel safe in calling you
two men to assist us in bringing the traitor to
justice, and if this is accomplished Andre may
be saved. Arnold must be captured at his quarters in New York. John Champ is to turn
traitor, desert his friends and join the British at
their gun-boats down by the harbor. The time
of his desertion is to be this evening at midnight. He is to have, if possible, an hour and a
half the start, before he is pursued by men who
will think his desertion is sincere. And you,
Foster," he continued, "are to head the Legion
and start after him. You must remember that
they will all think he is a deserter, that he is following the steps of Arnold, and the utmost caution must be taken by you to keep the men so
far behind him that pistol ball will not reach
him. Starting from here Champ will ride to
where the British ships are anchored, where he
will dismount and swim out to them. The
chase you will give will be observed by the British, and Champ will be welcomed by them as a
hero. He can then lay his plans for the capturing of Arnold."

After the plans had been deliberated and
talked over, until each of the gallant men perfectly understood the part he was to play, they
prepared to retire. Champ again wrapped him-

self in the cloak and passing the guard un-
recognized, made his way through the darkness
to his quarters. Foster also returned to his
comrades, leaving the horse with Lee's servant
to give color to the idea it had been presented
and accepted.

As midnight approached, Champ took stealthy
leave of his sleeping companions, and made
his way to a nearby thicket, where a little sorrel
mare was tied, already saddled and bridled. Un-
fastening her he led her forth, mounted and
started. The inside guards were passed in
safety. Then starting his steed into a gallop, he
rode rapidly towards the outposts. On the corner of a projecting rock stood a sentinel. As
the horseman approached, there rang out on
the clear night air the challenge: "Halt!—Who
comes there?" The aproaching horseman made
no reply. Again the challenge was repeated,
and again no reply. Still again the guard challenged, but on came the deserter, and crack
went the guard's rifle as the brave sergeant
passed by; a button was torn from his coat, so
close did the sentinel fire. But still he dashed
on and in another instant, ere the guard had
time to reload his flint-lock, he had disappeared
in the darkness.

The faithful picket immediately called for the

corporal of the guard, and reported the affair to him, telling him, that from the man's actions and his daring conduct, he believed that it was no less a person than Sergeant Champ, and that he believed he was deserting to the British. The corporal immediately reported to the officer of the day what the picket had told him, and that officer hastened to Lee's tent with pale face and bated breath. Lee had lain down. Answering his servant's summons, he arose and met the captain.

"Major," exclaimed the excited captain, forgetting in his excitement to salute, "a soldier has passed the pickets and gone to the enemy."

Lee first reminded the captain of his breach of etiquette, and then told him that the thing he reported must be a mistake. "There can not be," he said, "another Arnold among my men; impossible, sir."

"Yes it is, sir," answered the captain, "Sergeant Champ, the bravest man among us, has passed the lines on a horse and deserted to the enemy." "I don't believe it," answered Major Lee, "there must be a mistake somewhere. Go back and investigate it, and don't disturb me, for I wish to sleep." But the persistent captain was not to be put off. "I say, Major," he said, getting excited and impatient, "we are sure it was Sergeant Champ. He was on a horse, and going towards Paulus Hook. He paid no attention to the challenges of the picket, but seemed determined to pass." But again Major Lee said there must be some mistake. "I don't believe Champ would desert," said he, "leave me, for I want to get some rest and sleep after my hard ride of yesterday." And with this injunction Lee turned to go to his apartments. But the faithful captain would not be put off by even this; and so, after considerable delay, Lee gave orders to call the Legion together, and sent an orderly for Foster. The Legion assembled and Foster, putting in his appearance, Lee summoned him before the troopers. He told him that he, knowing the roads, was to lead the Legion in pursuit and gave him the black horse to ride, saying it was a good horse and Foster having captured and presented it to him, might have the honor of riding him first. When they were all ready to start, Lee shook his head doubtingly and again declared that he did not believe that it was possible that Champ could have deserted. Detaining the Legion again, he dispatched a messenger to Champ's quarters under pretense of making sure that he had really left the camp. While the messenger was gone Lee called Foster into his tent, and again went over with him the part he was to play in the ruse. Foster was to detain the troopers on the road as much as possible without causing suspicion. "Champ must not be overtaken," said Lee, "ride as near to him as is expedient, but for God's sake, and for the cause of our country, don't overtake him." Foster assured Lee that he would do his utmost to make the affair appear as it was intended that it should; while at the same time he would protect the life of Champ. They returned to the waiting men, who were in their saddles, anxious to be off. The orderly had returned, and now reported to Major Lee that Champ was missing from his place, and had undoubtedly deserted. Lee seemed satisfied at this report and convinced that Champ had deserted, he now seemed anxious that he be captured. He appeared so anxious that he detained the Legion another twenty minutes, giving further directions and suggestions as to the probable route taken by the deserter, and the course the Legion was to follow in pursuit of him.

At last all was ready, and at a few minutes past one o'clock, as long as he could well detain them, Lee saw the dragoons gallop off in hot haste after the supposed traitor. He returned to his couch and laid down, but not to sleep. His bravery and coolness on the battle-field could not be equaled, but the suspense he was now in was of a different nature. One of his bravest men was being pursued by his own comrades. They in their ignorance believing him to be a *traitor*, when in reality, no truer heart ever beat for the cause of American liberty.

CHAPTER IV.

BUT what of Champ and his pursuers? The former was mounted on a horse selected by Major Lee himself for its fleetness and endurance. But it was a little too light for a long and hard ride. He galloped easily along through the darkness, while behind him, but an hour's time between them, thundered the Legion in hot pursuit. They had gone through a number of small hamlets during the darkness, and as day dawned they were but a few miles north of the village of Bergen. As they came to the top of the hill they sighted Champ but three-fourths of a mile down the road, urging his little mare to the top of her speed. They set up a shout as they caught sight of him and clattered down the hill, feeling sure of capturing him at once, but he reached the top of an opposite hill and disappeared over the brow with all the speed imaginable.

On dashed the Legion, Foster on his black charger in the lead. They quickly covered the mile of road and reaching the top of the hill again saw Champ, rapidly approaching the village. Foster, by reason of his repeated excursions about the State, was familiar with the roads. He knew that if Champ could pass safely through the village, and cross a bridge at the outskirts, with but five minutes ahead of the Legion, he could successfully reach the shore opposite where the ships were probably anchored. He would then be safe from the infuriated members of the Legion, who were now spurring their horses to their utmost efforts, and were angrily declaring that they would shoot the traitor when they came within range of him, if he would not stop at their commands.

"This," said Foster in after years, when relating the tale to his family, "was the most trying experience of my life. My companions, believing that Champ was a traitor, were intent on either capturing or shooting him. How to prevent it, and give him the necessary start from the bridge, was what now occupied my mind with the liveliest kind of speculations and plans." As he rapidly revolved different schemes in his mind, he recollected that a short distance ahead a road branched off from the main one and connected with another, that joined the main road just below the bridge. By taking this they would go around the village while Champ would have a straight course through the town. He instantly resolved to throw his party temporarily off the track by taking this side road.

Accordingly as they came to it Foster reigned his black charger, which all the while had kept in the lead, into this side road; and the whole party followed. Not until they had gone quite a distance did any of the party discover the mistake. They halted and Foster, parleying with them as long as possible, finally persuaded them that it was the best plan to keep to the road they were on; and by doing so they might succeed in heading Champ off at the bridge. To this they finally agreed and started off again, eager to reach the bridge and capture the fleeing traitor. They came nearer capturing him than Foster had intended they should. As they neared the main road again below the village they caught sight of Champ riding furiously towards the bridge. The men of the Legion urged their steeds to their utmost; but lost sight of him as a hill hid the main road from them. Again they sighted him, and he was very near the bridge. With shouts of anger and yells to halt, they plunged their spurs into their horses' flanks, and made a final dash to head him off. Again a friendly hill hid him from their view, and from their pistols too, for they were preparing to fire. A moment later the clatter of his horse's hoofs on the bridge told them of his successful escape. With yells of enraged disappointment they dashed around the foot of the hill and on to the main road only to see Champ dashing away beyond the range of their pistols. They were now in sight of the harbor, and of the ships anchored a few rods from the shore. There was yet a possibility of overhauling him before he reached the shore, and they dashed on.

This finale of the chase was as successfully deceptive to the British on board the man of war, who were now watching the chase, as if every member of the pursuing party were aware of its true character. Foster, on his powerful black horse, led them furiously on, while Champ urged his nearly exhausted steed to a fearful gallop. Pistols were discharged at the fleeing sergeant, with hoarse shouts from the pursuers for him to halt or die.

On board the ships, the gunwales were lined with officers, while the British tars swarmed like rats up the rigging to observe the exciting chase. They soon perceived that the man on the sorrel horse was making for the ships, and that the party headed by the large man on the handsome black horse were eager to prevent it. So they cheered the fleeing man lustily, while the pursuers shouted back defiance and wrath.

Riding to the shore opposite the ships, Champ dismounted, hastily pulled off his heavy riding boots, and taking his sword in his teeth and his pistol in his hand, plunged into the river and struck out boldly for the ships. Even then, the members of the Legion thought to prevent his supposed desertion by his death. Riding up to the bank, they discharged their pistols at him as he swam. Fortunately for him, those hardy men did not have their muskets with them, for if they had he certainly would have been riddled with bullets. As it was, the water was splashed up all around him as the bullets struck its surface. But the men, not being used to pistols, fired very inaccurately, or otherwise the plucky sergeant would certainly have been killed. Foster, of course, fired wide of the mark. The British on the ships sent up a mighty shout of approval as Champ plunged into the river and struck out for the vessels. And when his pursuers began to fire at him, some of the officers hastily manned a gun to drive them back and protect the swimmer. One shot from the cannon sent them in haste from the bank to a safer place. There, with disappointment and chagrin, they watched until Champ reached the side of the nearest ship; a rope was thrown him and he was drawn on board, amidst the cheers of the officers and crews. Then they turned about and rode their well-nigh exhausted steeds to the village, where they stopped for a few hours' rest before the return to the army. The men of the Legion uttered many bitter expressions of surprise and denunciation at Champ's unexpected desertion. So good, so brave and apparently so true a man they never expected would be guilty of such detestable conduct as deserting to the enemy; yet he had, and they branded him a fit subject for the gibbet. And all agreed if ever he was captured, that that fate awaited him.

The magnificent black horse which had carried Foster at the very forefront of the party during the long and furious chase, had become slightly lamed by an injury to the frog of one of his forward feet; and under the pretense of giving the horse a longer rest, Foster remained in the village while the Legion returned to camp. What Foster really wanted was an opportunity to go down to the harbor that night and look for a message Champ had agreed to throw overboard at flood tide, if he could do so unobserved. When night came on Foster made his way to the shore opposite the ships. The moon was just rising and cast its pale beams on the rippling waves. as the tide forced them up the sloping bank. The ships, silent and majestic, rode at anchor at the same places they occupied in the morning. Foster walked down to the bank and seating himself, waited patiently for an hour, watching intently the water and waves along the shore.

Soon after he took his position on the shore he had heard a splash in the water as if something had been dropped overboard. But he had almost given up anything coming of it when he espied dancing on the little waves a few yards out a bit of firewood. Something of this kind was what he had been watching for, and he hastened to get it with the aid of a long pole. As he expected there was fastened to it a note addressed to Major Lee, in the handwriting of Champ. Placing the note in his bosom, he mounted his trusty horse and galloped away through the night to the camp of Major Lee. He willingly submitted to arrest by the sentinel on the outposts, and when brought before the officer of the day, he was sent at once to Major Lee, according to previous instructions from headquarters. He then delivered the note from Champ, and waited in silence while Lee eagerly read it. "So far, so good," remarked Lee, as he finished its contents.

Champ had been received by the British as

a hero. In his note he said he had been the lion
of the ship that day. During the few hours he
had been aboard, he had learned that Arnold
was to be put in command of a regiment of Loyalists, which was being raised in New York
City, and that he was sojourning there now.
Champ had decided to enlist in this regiment in
order to further his plans for capturing the traitor. The ship's commander had promised to
put him ashore next day, with a note of
recommendation to Arnold. This would aid
him in getting into the confidence of the traitor,
and bring him in personal contact with the very
man he wished to lay his hands on. He closed
his note with the request that Foster be allowed
on the following night to go to a certain spot
on the North river, about where Hoboken is now
situated. There he would endeavor to com-
municate with him again.

"Now, my good man," said Lee, as he finished telling Foster of what the note contained,
"all depends on his actions during the next few
days. This man Andre, who was captured with
Arnold's papers in his boots, may be saved, if
Champ is successful in capturing Arnold. I
will now give you a pass which will take you
through the lines at any hour of the day or
night." Receiving the pass, Foster withdrew

and went to his own quarters, where, after satisfying his hunger, he gave himself up to rest and slumber until mid-day. Then he arose and prepared to go to Hoboken.

Mounting the black horse, which had recovered from his lameness, he rode to the outposts, and showing his pass, started off down the highway for Hoboken. His ride was far different from the furious one he had taken less than forty-eight hours before. Then he galloped madly at the head of a party of angry men, plunging through the darkness, all but himself intent on capturing or shooting the traitor, Champ. Now he allowed his steed to canter easily along, observing with pleasing mood the beauties of the scenery presented by the surrounding country, which was just beginning to be tinged with the beauties of the autumal season. As he passed by the place where Champ had dismounted the day before and made his escape to the ships, he observed that they had weighed anchor and were gone. This pleased him. They had undoubtedly landed Champ and anchored farther out in the harbor. And on reaching the place Champ had told him to wait, what was his surprise to find the man-of-war securely riding at anchor, only a few rods from the very bluff Champ had designated as the meeting place.

5

What to do he did not know. But concluding to hold his position according to directions, he concealed his horse in a clump of trees and bushes, and as darkness settled over the river seated himself under the shadow of a huge rock and waited.

The nearness of the man-of-war made him fear that Champ would not dare to row to that point. Yet he hoped that as the darkness came on, he might. The ships were so near that he was obliged to exercise caution in concealing himself from any possible observers on the decks; while he could easily hear the voices of the sailors as they told their stories and sang their songs on the forward decks. He had watched and waited scarcely an hour, however, when he saw by the dim rays of the rising moon, a row boat propelled by a single oarsman, coming towards the bluff. The occupant was evidently a fisherman, for he was clad in a tar hat and oil coat. Several small nets suspended from poles, together with some fishing rods, hung over the bow of the skiff. The rower guided his boat under the very shadows of the frowning men-of-war, and coming to within a few rods of the bluff on which Foster was seated, dropped anchor and commenced to fish. And to an ordinary observer he did fish. But al-

though he cast industriously, he hooked nothing.
Foster from his seat by the rock, soon discovered that the fisherman was evidently trying to
cast his line on the shore instead of in the water;
and what was more peculiar, there seemed to be
an unusual kind of bait on the hook. Champ
(for it was he) had disguised himself and his
actions so well that even Foster had failed to
recognize him. Surmising now that it was
Champ, Foster gave a slight cough, which was
instantly answered by the occupant of the boat.

"Hist, cast a little farther," muttered Foster,
under his breath.

Champ heard him and casting a little farther,
landed, almost at Foster's feet, a small packet of
paper fastened to the end of his line. Detach-
ing it and casting the line into the water, Foster
stole away in the darkness, leaving Champ to
confirm the deception he was practicing upon
the British in the ships, by really fishing for half
an hour before returning to the New York
shore.

Long before a streak of day had appeared,
Foster had delivered the note to Lee. It stated
that Champ had seen Arnold and presented the
note from the naval commander. Arnold seemed
pleased to meet him, and had promised to give
him an important position in his regiment, when

they went south. After registering, Champ had been given his liberty; and he had improved it by finding the whereabouts of Arnold's lodgings. They were situated on the bank of the North river, and by interviewing an old darky servant of the place, he had learned that in the cool of the evening before he had retired for the night, Arnold was in the habit of walking in the garden of the place, which went down to the water's edge. Champ immediately conceived the idea of seizing Arnold some dark night as he was thus taking his evening promenade, and bundling him into a boat, convey him to a party waiting across the river.

All of these facts and plans Champ transmitted in his note to Lee. This was the first of several notes Champ sent to his commander by Foster, all of them cast ashore on a fish line and under the very nose of British gunboats. They would be most interesting and valuable now, if they had been preserved and could be given *verbatim*, but as far as we know they were not saved and we have only the traditions in the Foster family to depend on for their contents. Foster was on hand at the bluff the next night, and for several nights afterwards. Each time, under the guise of a fisherman, Champ rowed across the river under the prows of the men-of-war, and cast his communication to the waiting Foster.

Finally Champ gave the information that his plans were nearly matured, and asked that a posse be in waiting the next night, to receive the traitor he was now sure of capturing.

His plans as outlined in his various notes to Lee, are most interesting; and, if the traditions concerning them have beeen correctly preserved by the Fosters, are valuable additions to our histories of the war of the Revolution. They are to the effect that Champ made the acquaintance of a lady admirer of Major Andre, a sweetheart in fact. To her Champ made known his real character and his mission to capture and return to the American lines the traitor Arnold; telling her that if this was accomplished, he whom she admired and loved might be saved from the death of a spy. She, of course, instantly consented to aid him with all of her power, and soon enlisted in her services her colored male servant and a white man who was secretly a patriot.

Their plans were well laid, and on the night on which Champ had asked Lee to send a posse with Foster to Hoboken, they were to seize and gag Arnold as he took his usual walk in his garden, and hustling him into a skiff, were to row him across the river to the American army. Acting upon the request of Champ, Lee selected five trusted men, swore them to secrecy, and then revealed to them the plan, and sent them with Foster to the position designated by Champ, which was about a quarter of a mile north of the bluff he had been occupying for the past few nights.

All night long this little party watched up and down the river at Hoboken. The men-of-war had changed their positions, and anchored a mile away, lower down the harbor, so they were no longer to be feared. Yet the brave sergeant and his coveted prize did not appear. What could keep him? Had his plans failed? Had he been unsuccessful in his endeavors to capture Arnold? These and other like questions Foster and his companions asked each other the whole night long, as they patroled the shore and watched the river in the darkness. As day began to dawn they were forced to abandon all hope and concluded that Champ, in his attempt to seize the traitor, had been resisted and killed. Disappointed and disheartened, Foster and his companions returned to their camp.

What was the matter? That very day on which Champ had completed his well laid plans, and was waiting only for the night to carry

them out, Arnold had been ordered to prepare
to go with his regiment of Loyalists to Virginia,
and so did not go to his lodgings that night,
but remained at the quarters of his regiment.
Champ having enlisted in the same regiment,
was obliged to remain at the barracks too; so
that he could not even row out on his nightly
fishing excursion and apprise the waiting and
expectant party of the failure of his plans.

Had the order for Arnold's movement south
been delayed but twenty-four hours, the traitor,
in all probability, would have been captured,
and he, instead of Andre, would have been
hung, and that portion of our country's history
changed completely.

During the time Champ was in the British
lines it was not believed that he was suspected
of acting the part of a spy by either the British
or by his former comrades in the American
army. They both believed him sincere. He
was obliged to accompany Arnold's regiment
to Virginia, but at the very first opportunity deserted and made his way to Major Lee's corps,
which was then in the vicinity.

As he entered the lines he was greeted with
jeers and hisses, and finally was arrested and
marched off to headquarters. Foster was
standing in front of Lee's tent as Champ was

brought in. "My God," he exclaimed, as he caught sight of Champ between the guards, "I thought you lost or dead.

It was an affecting scene. The two stalwart men embracing each other with tears in their eyes; and as they stood there clasping each other's hands, they heard a noise at the tent door behind them. Turning they saw Major Lee approaching; again they saluted him together as they had done many months before. After acknowledging the graceful courtesy, Lee advanced and grasping Champ by both hands, welcomed him with tears streaming down his face. Not until this spectacle afforded them, did the guards and others standing about (many of whom figured in the exciting pursuit of Champ) suspect the true character and import of his desertion on that memorable night. Now they realized that it was some secret work that he had gone to do, and many a coat sleeve was drawn across the eyes as the hardy men recollected their angry chase and denunciatory expressions of opinion of him afterwards. They now crowded about the brave sergeant with greetings and apologies, extended in their rough but thoroughly sincere manner.

CHAPTER V.

LET us now return to that humble home in Hindsdale, New Hampshire, and see what was going on there while the husband and father was passing through the exciting scenes and incidents of the war, and enduring the privations and destitutions of the seven years' struggle for liberty. They lacked but little of being as hard at home and among the members of that patriotic family, as were the experiences of the loved one who was absent.

It will be remembered that Mr. Foster left for the seat of war on the first of February. He had seen to it that they were well supplied with food and fuel, enough to last them until spring. He had worked up a huge pile of wood, and corded it near the cabin, while corned and cured meat, such as pork, venison, and bear meat, enough for the winter, had been provided in the fall, so they lived fairly well. As the spring approached, Mrs. Foster began preparations to till the soil as best she could in the absence of her husband.

There were but few men in the whole township. The majority of them being away to war. All of the Tories, with the exception of the Wilson family, had removed to Boston. The few men that were left, however, generously gave such aid as they could to the families of the absent patriots. All but Wilson; he was still bitter against the cause of the Colonies: And "Billy" Wilson (as the people of the township called him) was anything but beloved by them. A kind neighbor of Mrs. Foster plowed her land. And with her own hands she planted the seeds. Corn and flax were sown, and potatoes planted. The older children worked with a will, and with the aid of their half-grown strength, she looked after the crops faithfully during the summer, harvesting them in good shape in the fall.

Elisha and Nat trapped and hunted incessantly. But their great drawback was the need of a good gun to shoot with. Their father owned two guns, but had taken the best one with him. The remaining one the boys would carry into the woods, and although unable to shoot without a rest, they would often be successful in bagging small game. The gun being a smooth bore, could not bring down any of the larger game they often had the opportunity of shoot-

"With the aid of their half-grown strength she looked after the crops."

ing. This, as can be readily imagined, was a great irritation to the boys, particularly when they would see a noble moose or deeer stalking serenely by them beyond the reach of their buckshot.

When, at length, they encountered a panther in a tall sycamore tree, and failed to bring it down with repeated shots from their smooth bore, their indignation knew no bounds. They immediately went to the town store, two miles away, and, manlike, contracted with the proprietor of the store for a *rifle*, to be paid for from the pelts and skins of such animals as they might shoot or trap. The boys obtained their precious gun by the middle of the summer, and then the deer, moose and other large game began to suffer. Even though they had not the strength of manhood, their marksmanship was accurate. Young Nat, who was but nine years old, was even a better shot than Elisha, who was two years his senior. And though he could not fire either gun without the recoil knocking him over, still he never failed to bring down his game. They soon had enough wild meat corned and cured to last them through the approaching winter. And this, with the successful harvesting of the crops, put all fears of a lack of food from Mrs. Foster's mind. But what gave

her the greatest anxiety, was the question of
clothing for her children. Their large flock of
sheep had been sadly depleted by the depredations of the Indians before Mr. Foster went
away; and the wool from the three or four remaining ones would not furnish enough material for socks for the family, to say nothing of
shirts, trowsers and jackets for the boys, and
dresses and petticoats for the girls. Her only
resource was to rough linen, made from the
flax she had grown. This she had cultivated
with great care, and safely harvested it. So
working it up from the rough, by the laborious
process of pounding, carding, spinning, and
weaving, she made passable clothing for her
brood of little ones.

As the autumn came, the boys turned their
attention to the working up of a supply of winter's wood. They would go into the woods and
chop down immense trees, and hitching their
ox team to the logs, drag them to the cabin,
where Mrs. Foster, herself, would aid them in
splitting and chopping them into sections of the
proper size for burning in their one fire place.
But although they prepared an immense amount
of wood, before the winter was half gone, their
supply was exhausted. Then the boys, in the
midst of the cold and stormy weather, would

work from day to day at wood chopping. In this occupation they resorted to a device for keeping their feet warm, which was both unique and original, and also shows their unprotected condition. They had no socks to protect their feet from the cold, only rude moccasins made by themselves from deerskin. So in order to keep their feet warm, and permit them to work at their wood chopping, without losing time to go beside the fire to get warm, they split a beech log into sections, five or six inches in thickness. Then hewing them down smooth with an ax, they would place them by the fire and heat them as much as possible without igniting them. To the choppers' yard one of the boys would then run out with one of the heated blocks and placing it on the chips, the one chopping would stand upon it while he worked. As it became cold, it would be replaced with one fresh from the fireplace. In this manner the boys worked on day after day, until gentle spring came again, and released them from their struggle with the cold. It is needless to say that after this experience the boys always laid in wood enough to last through the entire winter.

As each season came and went the children increased in size and strength, doing each year a greater amount of work for the common welfare of the family. The boys early attained their growth. Their muscles were knit into sinews of iron by their sturdy labor in field and wood, and by the time Elisha and Nat were fourteen or fifteen years of age, they easily did the work of men.

Many and varied were the experiences and adventures of these boys. Together they were the "head of the family" in the matter of working the farm and otherwise providing for the wants of all.

It was one summer day during the second year of their father's absence that they had their first and last serious difficulty with Indians. Previously they had been frequently visited by wandering red men, who would apply for something to eat, always helping themselves, if what was offered them was not satisfactory. They often carried away with them a considerable quantity of the family's supply of provisions, and there being no men around they were never resisted. They often compelled the boys to turn their grindstone for them to sharpen their knives and tomahawks, occasionally amusing themselves by threatening to tomahawk and scalp them. They would take hold of one of the children, and encircling its head with the back of a knife (after the manner of scalping) would show the trembling children how the thing was done.

On the occasion mentioned, a party of ten Indians came to the cabin and demanded venison and "fire water." The latter they did not have, but of the former, Mrs. Foster gave them a large piece she had already cooked for the household. They did not seem at all disposed to hurry away, but made themselves at home, making a meal of the haunch of venison and some corn bread Mrs. Foster had in the house. Elisha and Nat viewed these proceedings with ill-concealed contempt, and when they dispatched Nat to a spring to fill their jug with water, he went only out of sight of the cabin and filled it from a stagnant frog pond. While he was absent the Indians began to ransack the cabin for the barrels of venison they knew must be about, but also collecting whatever met their fancy. Elisha, whose indignation now knew no bounds, met Nat on his return and informed him of the Indians' doings. He, of course, became as mad as Elisha, and together they hurried to the cabin, determined to do something to stop the lawless proceedings. Going to the chief they commenced their angry protests. He paid no attention to their vehement language, however, but reaching out his hand, took the jug of water Nat had brought and placing it to his mouth, proceeded to take a long and deep draught. One gurgle of the foul water down his throat roused his wrath. Setting the jug down, he uttered a command in his own dialect to the others, and they seized Nat, bound him, dragged him from the cabin, and fastened him to a tree. Then brandishing their tomahawks, they danced about the fettered youth, who remained as stolid as one of their own chiefs in a war council.

But consternation filled the rest of the family. With a scream of terror, Mrs. Foster threw herself on her knees before the chief and besought him to spare her boy. He, still thinking of the undiscovered venison, told her he would release the boy for a good supply of that article. "Take it," said Mrs. Foster, "take everything, only spare my boy." She led the way to an outer cellar behind the cabin where the venison was concealed, and allowed them to help themselves. After doing so and nearly emptying a whole barrel in the process, they gathered up the clothing and blankets of skin they had collected and took their departure, leaving Nat still tied to the tree. He was released from his position by Elisha, and together the angry and incautious lads would have set out after the Indians with their guns if not restrained by their mother. Nat was so angered that he declared an Indian would never lay hands on him again and live; a threat which he fully verified in after life.

When chided by his mother for bringing stagnant water instead of fresh spring water to the Indians, and reminded by her of the nearly fatal results of his doing so, he declared that he did not care, that "frog water was good enough for the Injun whelps."

During the same summer, after this trouble with the Indians, the boys had a serious encounter with an old female panther. It happened in this wise. A bear was seen to cross the clearing surrounding the cabin one morning and disappear in the woods. They immediately abandoned the work they were engaged in, got their guns and started in pursuit. As the bear had a considerable start in the woods, they were obliged to follow him by trail. Following it quite a distance they observed, as they supposed, that the bear had suddenly changed its course, and started off at right angles to his former one. They immediately started in the new direction, with eager expectation of overtaking bruin. They went out a little ways before they did start up game; not the bear, but instead, an ugly old female panther, with two kittens under her maternal care. The kittens were not over two days old, and evidently had only just got their eyes open, and were out for their first promenade. The old panther sprang into a hemlock tree as the boys approached her lair, and lashing the boughs with her tail, prepared to spring upon them. A hasty, very hasty council of war was held by the young hunters. Elisha, who carried the old smooth bore, told Nat to fire first, while he would reserve his charge of buckshot for a contest at close range if it became necessary.

Nat accordingly took careful aim, using the side of a tree for a rest, and fired. The rifle, as usual, kicked him over, but a scream of pain from the panther told him that his bullet had reached its mark. Screeching with pain and fury, the panther scrambled to the very top of the tree and turned to spring, but fell to the ground. The boys shouted with joy, supposing she was dead. But not so—up she jumped the moment she struck the ground, and with long leaps made towards the boys. Elisha now aimed his smooth bore across the shoulders of Nat, who knelt down to afford his brother this rest, and fired into the very face of the panther, as he was scarcely twelve feet away. The peppery buckshot was effectual. With another leap she fell dead at their very feet. It was a narrow escape for the boys, but they were as cool and indifferent as mature men. Nat said he did not know which was worse, to shoot panthers or fight Injuns."

After skinning the panther, they looked around for the young ones and found them under the shelter of a huge rock, and mewing piteously for their mother. The boys took them home and kept them for some time; but as they grew larger and more playful, they also became more troublesome, so they were killed and the bounties for them obtained from the town. This bounty obtained for the slaughter of bears, wolves and panthers, though very small during the war, was about the only source of cash revenue the lads had, and the few shillings they obtained from the town in this way enabled them to keep going with tolerable fairness.

One night Nat started after the cows rather late, and being in a great hurry, did not stop to get a gun, as he usually did on going into the woods. The Fosters had no pasture fenced in. The land about the cabin whereon the crops were grown, was surrounded by a stone and log fence, and the herd was allowed to roam at will.

This evening they had wandered an unusual distance into the woods, and it was dusk before Nat located them by the tinkle of the bell on the leader. He rounded them up at once and started them off home at a brisk walk. They seemed somewhat frightened and loath to proceed, which immediately aroused Nat's suspicion that a wolf or panther had driven them into the woods, and was probably now lurking about. They had proceeded but a little ways on the homeward path ere his suspicions were confirmed by a monstrous panther, with its usual scream, springing from a tree, directly for the cow leading. He missed her, however, and disappeared in the brush. The frightened cows now started on a run, their terror increased by Nat's hallooing and shouting for somebody to bring a gun. The family heard him, and Elisha started, staggering under the weight of both the smooth bore and rifle. He met Nat at the bars in the fence, and Mrs. Foster and the girls taking charge of the cows, the boys returned to the woods and commenced to hunt for the panther. But although they went a long distance into the woods and were beyond the cow path, not a sign of a panther did they see. Giving it up at last, they turned their steps homeward. Darkness had now fallen upon them, and they had only the moon to lighten their path. As they approached the bars again, Nat espied what looked very much like a rock or boulder moving among the stones scattered about the fence and bars. "Hist," said he, "there's the painter," at the same time raising his rifle and firing. With one of its blood-curdling screeches the panther bounded to the top of the wall. There it stood but an instant, crouching upon the stones, angrily lashing its yellow sides with its tail, its agile form dimly outlined by the feeble rays of the moon, showing the devil's own look in its eyes. Elisha was a lad of deliberate action, and probably if Nat had waited for him to shoot, one or both of them would have been seriously injured by the now furious animal. But Nat was not of the slow moving kind, but quick as a flash, as his conduct now showed; springing to his feet, for the rifle had kicked him over, as usual, he snatched the smooth bore from his brother's hands and sent its charge of buckshot between the glaring eyes of the panther, and with another scream and a mighty leap into the air, it fell dead.

It had evidently followed the fleeing cows and shouting boy to the edge of the forest, and there lurked about, only kept from attacking the cows by the women's voices, as they got them into

their proper enclosure and prepared to milk
them. The boys, not expecting to find it so
near the cabin, had passed it as they went into
the woods. And only Nat's eagle eye detected
it on their return from the search in the woods.

One night the family was awakened by the
violent squealing of the pigs, which for greater
safety were kept in a sty near the cabin. Nat,
without stopping for the ceremony of dressing,
seized the rifle and made his way out into the
night. There was a bright moon, and he instantly discovered an immense black bear making off with one of the half grown pigs in his
embrace, the latter piercing the clear night air
with its lusty squeals. How to shoot the bear
without killing the pig at the same time was
Nat's first thought. But as the bear was rapidly
escaping, he dismissed this from his mind and
started in pursuit, the tails of his tow shirt flying
in the gentle breeze. Coming to within what he
would call a "healthy distance," he fired. With
a groan the bear fell in a heap, the pig underneath, and the sudden cessation of its agonized
squeals told him that if he had not shot it, its
life had certainly been crushed out by the weight
of the bear.

Bruin proved to be wounded in the shoulder.
Rising on its hind legs it immediately showed

fight. At this Nat, having no ammunition with him, shouted to the members of the family to bring him the powder horn and bullet pouch. The deliberate Elisha had stopped to don his trowsers and load the smooth bore. He now appeared with that favorite fowling piece in his hands, accompanied by little Solomon carrying the powder and balls.

A grotesque scene met their eyes, and convulsions of laughter seized them. Elisha, with his characteristic manner, sat down on a log, and commenced to hug himself as a paroxysm of laughter laid hold of him, while Solomon shouted to the family to "come quick and see Nat and the bear dance." There was the bear, reared on its hind legs, bending over the body of poor pig, growling fiercely and pawing the air with its one good fore paw, endeavoring to land a blow at Nat; the latter was dancing about him, his bare legs flashing in the moonlight, giving the bear an occasional blow on the head with the butt of the rifle, or a poke in the ribs with the end of the barrel. The rear tail of his shirt was trailing on the ground behind him, fastened to the garment proper by a single shred, it having been nearly torn off by the bear's landing a blow on his rear as he careened around its crouching body. This kind of sport did not suit Nat; neither did the amusement he was affording his brothers, on account of his position and appearance soothe him. But he did not cease an instant to engage the bear's attention. He continued to parry with him as industriously as ever, while he shouted to Elisha to let the bear have the charge in his gun.

"Shoot 'em, 'Lish, shoot 'em, I tell you," said he. "Stop your laughin' and shoot 'em," he exclaimed, growing more excited as he dodged a blow aimed at him by the bear and gave the brute a savage poke in the side with the gun, which nearly pushed the animal over.

"Lo-lo-look out for you legs, Nat," exclaimed Elisha, "he'll claw em." And he went off into another fit of laughter, without apparently having heard Nat's appeal to him to shoot.

"Nat, if you don't look out, he'll tear your best shirt offen you," said little Solomon, as he danced about at a safe distance from the dancing bear and hopping youth.

"You shet up and gimme that powder," retorted Nat, now thoroughly disgusted with the conduct of his brothers.

"Well, come and get it then," said Solomon, holding it out at arm's length, cautiously keeping at a safe distance from the contesting bear and boy, "I aint going to give him a chance to tear my shirt."

Nat seized the proffered horn, poured a charge into the gun, and, forgetting in his excitement to put in a ball, fired point blank into the bear's face.

"O-O-Oh!" shouted Elisha, "tha-tha-that only scorched his eyebrows," and he went off into another fit of laughter.

It was true that the charge of powder had scorched the bear's eyebrows; but it did more. It burned his nose, blinded his eyes, and greatly increased his fury. Dropping on his three legs (the fourth had been shattered by Nat's first shot) he limped blindly, but with wonderful rapidity towards the seated Elisha, who was again hugging himself and swaying his body back and forth, Nat's powder charge having tickled him so. But a shout of warning from Nat and his little brother, brought him to his senses. Ceasing his laughter, he looked up, and gazed almost directly in the wide open jaws of the enraged bear, as it was making towards him. Then for the first time, he realized that the struggle that had afforded them so much amusement, was of a really serious nature, and rousing himself to action, he seized the ever ready smooth bore, which until now had rested at his feet, and gallantly met the charge of the on-coming bear. It was already almost upon

him. Without putting the gun to his shoulder,
he thrust the muzzle into the bear's mouth and
fired the contents of the gun down its throat.
With a growl, a snort and a wheeze from his
lacerated windpipe, the poor beast gave up the
gallant fight it had been maintaining, and laid
down and died.

Although the family could ill-afford to lose
the pig, yet they estimated that they got more
meat from the bear's carcass, (which was a large
one), than they would have gotten from the
pig had they been enabled to fatten it. So bar-
ing the damage of Nat's tow shirt, the night's
adventure was a clear gain.

The boys once caught an eagle in a trap set
for wolves. The trap was fastened to a drag or
small log, in order to allow a wolf caught in it
to pull himself about a little. Often a wolf
caught in a trap securely fastened to a tree or a
log he could not move, would deliberately chew
his foot off and thus make his escape. In order
to avoid this, the boys always set their wolf traps
fastened to a small billet of wood, which would
admit of the animal's slow progress through the
woods after being caught. They were always
able to track and overtake him by means of the
trail made by the drag.

The eagle caught was a large and powerful

one, and would rise into the air the length of
the chain fastened to the trap, even lifting from
the ground one end of the small log to which
it was fastened; but the weight was too great
to admit of his flying away.

Nat was the one to discover the bird in the
trap, and he immediately rushed into a close
contest, intent on subduing and taking the eagle
alive. He as quickly retreated, however, and it
would be supposed a sadder and wiser boy. The
eagle, with its one free foot, its beak and wings,
gave him such a clawing, pecking and beating
that, when he presented himself at the cabin to
report the eagle in the trap, and secure assistance in capturing it, the family hardly knew
him. His tow shirt had fared worse than in his
memorable encounter with the bear. It was,
in fact, nearly torn from his body. His trowsers were a sight to behold; while blood
streamed from his nose, and from numerous
cuts and scratches on his face and shoulders.
He staunched the flow of blood at the wash
basin, while he related to the family his encounter with the eagle.

Meanwhile Elisha bustled about, procuring
ropes, an ax, and the trusty smooth bore, in
case they found it necessary to shoot the bird.
Nat, having stopped the flow of blood, washed

his face, pinned up his clothes with what was his ever ready fasteners, thorns, started with his brother to secure the bird. Having arrived, they decided after discussing the situation, that the free leg of the eagle must be first captured and bound to the one in the trap. Nat accordingly formed a slip noose in one of the ropes, and again rushed in on the powerful bird. One would naturally think that his former treatment from it would have taught him a lesson. But it apparently had made no impression on his mind, though it had on his body. For a few moments he and the eagle were hopelessly mixed. Feathers filled the air; clothes were ripped afresh; the thorn pins flew in every direction, while the eagle screamed with rage and fury, and Nat yelled lustily, probably more from the same cause than from the hurts he was getting. At last he laid a firm hold on the free leg of the bird, but in the struggle he had dropped the rope. However, he would not let go, not he. He continued his tussle until he landed the bird on its back; then he shouted to Elisha to get a forked stick and pin its head to the ground. Elisha seized the ax and plunged into the brush to cut the desired article, but as usual in cases of excitement and hurry, he could not readily find a stick with the proper crotch.

Meanwhile, Nat had unwarily released with one hand his grasp and reached out to get the rope lying near. Whereupon the eagle renewed its struggles. Again they fought, the bird sometimes on top, terribly beating the lad with its wings; the next instant Nat on top endeavoring to throw the bird down. But again he mastered it, and Elisha at last appearing with the stick, succeeded in fastening its head to the ground by placing the forks of the stick across its neck, thus effectively shutting off its wind. Then it was an easy matter to bind its legs, and a cord around its throat kept up the "shutting off" process on its windpipe; thus the bird was conveyed home and laid at the cabin door, admired by the whole family. The boys constructed a cage of poles and kept the bird captive the rest of the summer. Its leg, broken by the trap, soon healed and it grew quite tame, and would cackle and scream in the morning for its breakfast of fresh meat, which the boys, by their hunting, always had in abundance. They named the pet "Old Put" in memory of Gen. Putnam, with whose fame they were familiar.

Old Put was, of course, a great favorite with the whole family, but he soon became a troublesome one. He proved very destructive to their hens and chickens. The cunning bird would stand near the bars of his cage, his broken leg drawn up under his body, his eyes drooping and nearly closed, and to all appearances sound asleep. But let an unwary chick come within range of his beak,—quick as a flash he would thrust his head through the bars, seize the unfortunate fowl by the neck, and drawing it into his enclosure, quickly dispatch it. So Old Put was finally given his liberty. The boys particularly disliked to part with him, for they had fought to hard for his capture to let him go without regrets. But when the door of his cage was opened, he gladly availed himself of the opportunity to take his flight, and they watched him as he sailed away towards the mountains, finally becoming to them but a tiny speck against the blue sky.

But the liberation of Old Put was not the last seen of him, however; one day early in the following spring, they observed an immense eagle hovering about their clearing, and soon discovered by his crooked leg it was Old Put. They were all delighted, and the boys rejoiced; but when he carried off a number of their barn yard fowls and two of their spring lambs, they were forced to pocket their sentiment and shoot him. Thus was the interesting career of Old Put brought to a melancholy and untimely end.

Every person has a romance in his life, and Nat's had its beginning during this period of his life, though it did not culminate until he had attained man's estate.

We have spoken of "Billy Wilson," as the plain towns people called their aristocratic and Tory townsman; we have also spoken of the daughter of Mr. Wilson, whom he sent to Boston to school. She was his only child, and the pride of his heart. During the periods she was at home, she in some way made the acquaintance of Nat, and formed a deep attachment for him. She was a year or two his senior; but as he was a strong and healthy lad, he became her constant companion and protector in her rambles and strolls in the woods and fields for berries, acorns and nuts. He could climb the highest trees and go out on the most dangerous branches to shake down the nuts for her. While he knew the best berry patches and the choicest places to gather wild grapes and mandrakes. Little Mary was with Nat so much that her father became quite attached to the lad, and probably if his father had not been a patriot, would have made more of the boy. One time, after Mary had spent the winter and spring at school in Boston, she returned home with her mind filled with plans of berrying, nutting and rambling with Nat Foster. As soon as she arrived home, her first inquiry was in regard to Nat; and the next morning she put on a sunbonnet, took a splint basket on her arm, and called to see Mrs. Foster, incidently to see if Nat could go berrying with her. Nat was glad to see her, of course, and it was readily arranged that he might accompany her to where there were some luscious blackberries, he had discovered only the day before.

Taking the rifle, Nat started away with Mary at his side. She was full of news of her school life in Boston; and she entertained him with her stories and accounts of her life in Boston, until they had nearly covered the distance to the berry patch. Finally she began to question him in regard to his own school life, and was shocked and horrified to find that Nat could not even read. There were no schools maintained in the township, and the truth was, the children were growing up in ignorance. Little Mary had never discovered this defect in her admired friend. Summer after summer he had been playmate and companion, winning her respect and admiration by his feats of daring and skill, but she had never thought of Nat's mental accomplishments. For an instant she was shocked and grieved at this monstrous gap between her

and her chosen friend. Then a bright idea struck
her active brain.

"Why Nat," said she, "why don't you go to
Boston to school?"

"Go to Boston to school!" exclaimed Nat;
"why how is a fellow going to get the money to
pay?"

"Oh, I have it," answered Mary, "I'll ask my
father to pay for you. He will, I know, for he
likes you, and thinks you will make a nice man."

Just then they rounded a bend in the path
which brought them to the berry patch. But
it also brought them face to face with an old
she bear, with two cubs following. They were
lumbering along the path directly towards the
children. Mary screamed at the sight and clung
to her boy protector.

Said Nat: "Mary, you run and I will stay and
fight them off." But still she clung to her protector, and began to cry. Meanwhile the old
bear had continued towards them, until she was
but a few feet away. Having her cubs with her
she undoubtedly acted more fierce than she
would otherwise have done. She now sat upon
her haunches and began to growl fiercely, so
that even Nat began to be afraid. He kept his
eye fastened on the bear, however, while he
backed away, pushing his girl companion along

7

behind him, telling her all the while to run. Finally she did flee, and with all the swiftness her young strength permitted. Then Nat began to back off more rapidly, when the old bear dropped on all fours again, and ambled towards him. When she again drew near him she sat upon her haunches again. Nat redoubled his efforts to back away, when again the bear dropped upon all fours and trotted nearer, then she sat up again. This sort of game was kept up quite a distance down the path, Nat being restrained from shooting by the fact that he had no ammunition with him, save the charge in his gun.

Finally in his backing off process, Nat struck his foot against a root, and came near falling in a heap. In saving himself, he took his eyes off the bear, and as he struggled about to regain his footing, she made a rush for him. He took aim as well as he could (for he knew this was his only chance) and fired, and then turned and ran as he never ran before; in fact, it would have been a hard matter for the bear, if she was so disposed, to overtake him.

Nat soon overtook his little friend, who was nearly dead from fright and hard running. He soothed her as best he could, and then accompanied her home. When they arrived, Mary insisted that he go in, and she told her father of his gallant conduct. Mr. Wilson listened and when she had finished said:

"Well, I always knew the lad was a brave one, but then his father is a rebel, and I have no use for such people. But see here, my lad," he continued, turning to Nat, "if you will promise me to become a Loyalist I will send you to Boston to school, and make a gentleman of you."

Schooling was what Nat wanted, and here was the very opportunity that he and Mary had been talking about. But the insinuation thrown upon his father, together with the proposition of his turning Loyalist roused his indignation.

"What," said he, "I a Loyalist, and my father fighting for freedom? No! not for all the learning there is in Boston! If my dad is a rebel, then I'm one too." And with his face burning with wrath and indignation he stalked out of the house, without even stopping to bid Mary good bye. He went home and told his mother of his adventure, and his subsequent treatment at the hands of Mr. Wilson.

"Natty," said the good woman, "you have done right, and God will reward you for your good deeds, even if our fellow-men will not." And with this sentiment, and his mother's kind words, Nat was entirely satisfied.

The next morning he and Elisha went to the berry patch and found the bear dead. Nat's one shot had done its work. They also found the half grown cubs of the dead bear contentedly eating berries in the neighboring berry patch. Securing these they spent the remainder of the day getting the pelts and carcasses home, and trying out the fat of the cubs.

Nat had no opportunity to see his little friend Mary again. For her father would not permit it; and in the fall they moved to Boston, so that little Mary Wilson was soon forgotten, until an incident in his after life served to bring her memory to him again, together with her Tory father's unkindness. But this will be given in its proper place.

CHAPTER VI.

IN 1782, the war being about over, Mr. Foster decided to return to his home and fireside. I stop and lay down my pen as I attempt to describe that return to his home, and the reunion with his family.

Seven years and ten months he had been absent, fighting for the freedom of that country he loved as his own life. During those years he had received no word from or about his family. Whether they were living or dead he knew not. What success or failure they had had in keeping together, and securing a living, he had no idea, save that if his faithful spouse was living, she was doing all possible to keep the family together. He knew his children must be grown beyond his recognition. But of the condition of each and all he was entirely ignorant.

During the long period he had been in the Continental army he had not slept in a bed or eaten a meal decently cooked. He stood the strain well. His huge frame and iron constitution seemed proof against the severe hardships he had been called upon to endure. But still it

told on him towards the last. His form became
bent, and his face furrowed. Early in 1782 he
contracted a severe cold, which brought on inflammation of the eyes, and he was obliged to
go to one of the army surgeons for treatment.
At regular intervals attacks of ague also racked
his gigantic frame. His friends and the surgeon
attending him tried to persuade him to give up
and go home. But no, he would not leave the
army until England was whipped and his country free. So he continued in the field, suffering
from sore eyes, and his body shaken with ague
fits, until steps were taken to form the treaty of
peace; then he consented to give up, and immediately set his face homeward.

The same state of ignorance and suspense was
endured by his family during his protracted absence. As we have seen, they met, fairly and
successfully, the trials of their situation. Fortune smiled on Mrs. Foster and gave the children healthy bodies and willing hands to work
and endure for the common interest.

Providence was remarkably kind to them in
bestowing success upon their cultivation of the
soil and pursuit of the chase. The all seeing
and all powerful One had preserved and pro-
tected them. But year after year came and
went, and no word was received from the ab-

sent husband and father. The children frequently spoke of him, and Nat and Elisha often expressed the wish that "Father might see the excellent shot," or the "big game" brought home.

As time wore away, Mrs. Foster's face became more grave, and even sad. The children, sometimes noting it, asked the cause, but the noble woman seldom saddened their young hearts by telling them the real cause. Occasionally, however, she could not conceal her emotions. One day when Nat found her weeping, he guessed for the first time that she, fearing never to see his father again, had given him up as lost; and he, too, became thoughtful and sad for a time. But, boy-like, his exuberancy of spirits soon made him cheerful and lively again.

His mother, as we can well imagine, was an untiring worker. She managed their little farm so well that in a few seasons it was in a superior state of cultivation for those times. The stock was increased; the three or four sheep they had when Mr. Foster went away had multiplied to a large flock. A half a dozen of milch cows and a yoke of oxen, which the boys had raised and broken from calves, were among their possessions. When we think of the work that was done then by hand in the home, which is now performed by machinery in mills and factories, we wonder that the good woman was able to keep up at all, with the countless demands upon her. But her hands were willing and her ingenuity a resourceful one; and she worked on, constantly and bravely.

Let us glance at some of her presumably numerous duties. In the summer she had the crops to look after, the cows to attend, with the working up of their products. Under her direction the wild and domestic meats must be corned and cured for winter's use. In the fall she must superintend the harvesting of the crops; the cutting, rotting, pounding and working up of the flax, from which a large part of their supply of cloth was obtained. This task of properly securing the flax was no small one. It was first pulled and allowed to remain in the fields until the outer shell or bark had rotted away, then it was gathered and beaten up with a "pounder." The inner texture was then obtained for the work of the hetchel, card, spinning wheel and loom. Those familiar with the old-fashioned Herrick's Almanac, or who have been curious enough to examine the cuts that appear in that old free medical work, must have noticed a picture illustrating the process of pounding and working up of flax.

"She would set her spinning-wheel to running."

The carding of this beaten flax, together with the wool sheared from their sheep in the spring, must have occupied her attention well on into the winter. Then she would set her spinning wheel to running, and spend the winter in spinning and weaving.

It was while engaged in this occupation of spinning one day in November that her thoughts reverted to her absent husband. She was alone in the cabin. Zilpha, now a healthy and vigorous girl of fourteen, was working some fall butter in a little cabin by the spring. The boys had built it for a "milk house," but nowadays it would be dignified with the name of "creamery." The three younger children were in the woods gathering nuts.

There had been some very pleasant Indian summer days, which had greatly cheered this faithful woman. But this day the weather was of that bleak, autumnal character, which prevails most frequently during the month of November. The wind roared and howled through the tree tops, and moaned and sighed in its careerings down the chimney. Fitful gusts set the ashes in the fireplace flying through the air; and handfuls of dead leaves beat against the panes of the little window of the cabin, which incessantly rattled and shook in its casement.

Her state of mind was in keeping with the moaning and sighing wind and the melancholy droning of her spinning wheel. She felt mournful and disconsolate. But two months more would come and go, ere eight years would have passed since she had seen her husband. Vivid in her mind now was the scene of his parting, as he kissed her and the children good-bye and started, gun in hand, for Boston, to fight for freedom. She had heard months ago of the surrender of Cornwallis, and of the probable speedy termination of the war. Already, she had heard, the patriots were returning to their homes and hearth-stones. But would her husband return to her? Nay; she dare not hope that. Tears came to her eyes, but she resolutely dashed them away, and set her wheel to revolving more rapidly than ever. Soon came a knock. She stopped her wheel and going to the door, opened it. There stood before her a blear-eyed man, his clothing in rags, his long hair matted and snarled, his face unshaven, and his body painfully bowed. He lifted his watery eyes to her with a longing and beseeching look in them; but he spoke no word. She, supposing him to be a poor wayfarer, said, "Come in, my good man, and warm yourself, and I will give you a bite to eat." She moved aside and he stepped into the cabin. Straightening himself with an effort, he spoke for the first time:

"Lydia," said he, "don't you know me?"

She halted, she hesitated an instant, and then with a heaving breast and tears welling to her eyes, she clasped her husband to her bosom. Together they wept like children. His body was weak from sickness, and, fatigued by his long journey, gave way under the excitement and strain. He would have fallen had not his wife supported him, and guiding him to a chair seated herself, taking him on her lap, as she would one of her children. It was many moments before either could speak. And then Mrs. Foster could only cry out between her sobs of joy, "Oh, Nathaniel, Nathaniel, my husband, my husband."

"Lydia," said Mr. Foster at last, rousing himself, our country is free. Where are the children."

The mention of the children reminded Mrs. Foster that there were others to share her joy. Going to the door, she took down the dinner horn, and blew a loud and long blast from its metallic throat. Its summons at that unusual hour, was heeded at once by those within its sound, and caused them to hasten homeward, with all the speed possible.

The first to arrive was Zilpha. She was a beautiful girl, already developing into womanhood. She came running in great haste, carrying the wooden butter ladle she had been using, and which, in her hurry, she had forgotten to leave.

"Your father has come," was the simple announcement of her mother, as she met her at the door. With a cry of joy the girl sprang to the door, and then hesitated, gazing timidly at the ragged, unkempt man seated by the fire. There she stood bare-headed, her dark hair falling in ringlets about her shoulders, mantled with a simple dress of "homespun," her black eyes flashing, and her cheeks flushed from her run from the milk house, a most beautiful and welcome picture to her father.

"Come, my daughter, come," said Mr. Foster, holding out his hands to her. She hesitated no longer, but throwing the butter ladle upon the floor, sprang into the embracing arms of her poor father, and covered his weather-beaten face with her sweet kisses.

The children now came trooping in with their bags and baskets of nuts. They too, approached their father slyly. All but Sybil. She only stopped to ask, "Is that my pa you told me about?" and upon being told by her mother that it was her "pa," she exclaimed, "Then I will go and kiss him," and running to him, she threw her chubby arms about his neck and again rejoiced his heart by her caresses.

The boys soon arrived, bearing between them, slung to a pole, a yearling deer they had shot. The strapping young fellows were more noisy and boisterous in their greetings of their father than were the other children. Nat particularly was very demonstrative: "Hurrah for father," he shouted, as he tossed up his hat, and rushed into the cabin. "Hurrah, father," he shouted as he grasped his parent's hand. "Did you whip the Crown? he exclaimed, as he recollected the avowed object of his father's leaving home and which now seemed so many, many years ago. "Yes, yes, my lad," answered Mr. Foster, "we've fought the Crown, and beat him, too. Our country is now free, thank God."

The sight of his family grouped about him, with little Sybil on his knee, again moved Mr. Foster to tears of joy. Here they all were, safe and sound, well and healthy after his long absence from home.

The two oldest boys were strapping big fellows for their ages. Elisha was eighteen, and Nathaniel, though but sixteen, was fully as large as his elder brother. Zilpha was fourteen.

The next, Ann, was twelve. Solomon no longer considered himself little at the age of ten, though Sybil was content to be the baby of the family at eight.

Mr. Foster had gone unflinchingly through the dangers and hardships of war; he had participated in bloody battles, and seen with indifference loathsome acts of savagery. But these noble sons and daughters, standing before him, with their faithful mother, quite unnerved him, and he shed tears of gratitude and joy.

Regaining somewhat his composure, he blessed them all, as he had blessed them years before. The sense of strangeness which the children first felt towards their father soon wore away, and the boys began to tell him of their adventures and experiences in hunting and trapping, in working and managing the farm, in trading and bartering. He listened with keen relish and appreciation. Rousing himself, he went out and inspected the deer they had brought in; and then looked over the farm and stock, expressing great surprise and pleasure at the good and orderly appearance of everything. Returning to the house, they found the evening meal prepared, and with grateful hearts they gathered around the board, and bowed their heads as Mr. Foster—as the head of the household—invoked God's blessing on the meal. It was truly a happy family gathered around the table that night.

Supper being over, Mr. Foster again took Sybil on his knee and listened to the boys as they continued the accounts of their life during his absence. When pressed to tell his own experiences, he shook his head, and said:

"Not to-night, boys. Our country is free and you ought to be satisfied with that."

Not for weeks would Mr. Foster give his family any particular account of his years of wandering and fighting. He seemed so satisfied and thankful for his return home, and the finding of his family safe and sound, that he did not appear to care about mentioning any of his own experiences, but seemed contented and satisfied in listening to accounts of theirs, particularly those of the boys. He laughed long and loud as Solomon described Nat's nocturnal encounter with the bear, and the damage done to his tow shirt. He nodded his head approvingly when they told him of the capture, liberation, and subsequent shooting of Old Put. But he grew wrathy when they told him of the Indians' treatment of Nat in tying him to a tree. He at once fell to giving the boys some instruction and

advice on Indian hateing and Indian shooting.
Advice and instruction they did not need to
have impressed upon them so very much by
reason of their own encounters and experiences
with the savage men.

Under the benign influence of his home and
its comforts, Mr. Foster rapidly regained, to a
considerable degree, his former health, though
it was not possible that it be fully restored after
the long and severe strain on his constitution.
He was afterwards always afflicted with rheu-
matism; and his eyes troubled him, until finally
he became totally blind, from the effects of the
inflammation in them while in the army. Within
a few weeks after his return, however, he was
sufficiently restored to walk about the town,
bearing himself with pardonable pride, con-
scious, as he was, of his long and faithful service
in fighting for the freedom of the Colonies.

About this time he began to talk more freely
of his experiences and adventures while away
to war. And in this connection there was one
thing which seemed of particular interest to
him; that was the Mohawk Valley, and the surrounding country of hills and mountains covered with dense forest. The time of his campaign in New York State was when the country
was to be seen at its best. The noble hills and

broad valleys were luxuriant with their mantles of green. The Dutch settlements gave complete testimony of the fertility of the river meadows, while the forests of the adjacent hills and mountains abounded with game, which the patriot troops constantly bagged for food.

Mr. Foster so frequently spoke of the superiority of New York State to New Hampshire, that Nat surprised him one day, as he was drawing comparisons between the mountains of New York and of their own, by exclaiming, "Say father, let's go there and live." Mr. Foster looked at his swarthy son to see if he was in earnest, and being assured, he told the impulsive lad to be content where he was. That a bird in the hand was far better than two in the bush, and such like advice. Yet the suggestion of his son left its impression on his mind. Yes, why not go? Why not go west, as New York was then called? His family, which had been so mercifully preserved to him, were now at the time of vigorous youth, and demanded a better place for maturing than Hinsdale afforded. His farm, which they had kept up, was small, and the game, according to the boys' own testimony, was already beginning to disappear. Yes, why not go?

He broached the subject to the family, and the idea was hailed with delight by the boys. Only Mrs. Foster, with the characteristics of her sex, was loath to leave the old place. But the matter being fully discussed as the winter advanced, it was definitely settled that they should go in the spring. After all, Nat's suggestion prevailed. We shall see, as we follow his life, what an important bearing it had on his career.

And so now, after years of fighting and warring, the old patriot was to see a new home. As in the prime of life he had left Rhode Island and sought a home in New Hampshire, for that family that was to be born to him; so now, in his older years, he was to seek a more congenial place for the family to develope in, which would admit of their expansion. Already he felt the weight of years. His constitution, once as of iron, was now broken and shattered; and added to this was threatened blindness.

And here I would pause and relate a touching incident connected with the darkness of his last days, at the risk of being censured for interpolating. It happened many years after his emigration to New York State, (1826), when he was spending the quiet of his extreme old age with his son, Nat, at the latter's home in Salisbury, Herkimer county, N. Y. A reunion of the Fosters was being held at Nat's home, and among the guests was a lad of seven years, a great-grandson of Mr. Foster.

The old man, in the weakness of his age, was lying on a bed in a room adjoining that in which the company were assembled. He heard them speaking of this boy in very flattering terms. They all regarded him as a child of great promise. Hearing them speak so much of the boy, he requested that he be brought to him. So, agreeably to his request, the lad was brought in to his bedside. The old man proceeded to give him such advice, in regard to his duty to his God, his country and his fellow-man, as he, by reason of his ripe age and matured experience, was so well fitted to give. And then rising to a sitting posture, he stretched out his hands and laid them upon the boy's head, and raising his sightless eyes to heaven, like Jacob of old, gave the lad his patriarchal blessing.

It was a touching episode, and one which moved all of the witnesses as they were grouped around the blind and aged patriarch, and the fair young child. It left its lasting impression upon the heart of the lad. He still lives (1897) at an advanced age in one of the northern towns of Fulton County, N. Y. His life has been a fulfillment of the prophecies his relatives made of him that day, and impressed and emphasized by his grandsire's advice and blessing. And his own testimony is to the effect that that advice and blessing did much to mold and fashion his life into the one of virtue, honesty and devotion to God, which has characterized it.

The above incident will also suffice as a refutation of the story that is sometimes heard in the woods in connection with the life of Nat Foster, the son. It is to the effect that his father, mother, brother, and sisters were all massacred at one time by the Indians. The elder Foster died peacefully at the home of Nat, soon after the above incident.

The children were all eager to go into the new country. Nat was particularly anxious to go; for the advantages he was sure it would afford him and Elisha for hunting and trapping.

"Are there any Injuns there dad?" he innocently asked his father one day, as they were talking over the plans of moving in the spring.

"Injuns!" exclaimed his father, starting up, "Injuns, did you say? Yes, lots of 'em. And you'll have need to look out lad, if you go to hunting and trapping in the mountains north of the valley. The red devils will steal you blind.

and then kill you in the bargain." And he continued giving his young son more advice and information about Indians and Indian fighting.

"I'll tell what, my lad," he said, "make shooting the red devils your life's work. But even then," he continued, "you can't repay 'em for half the hellish work I've seen 'em do right in that valley since I've been away. Never excite a quarrel with any of 'em," he went on, "or with any one, for that matter. Be kind and as peaceful as you can, for that's what our Maker intended us to be. But," he added, with a grim snapping of his jaws, "it's different with them cussed Injuns. You can't be peaceable with 'em nohow."

Of all the experiences or accounts of his adventures he would give concerning his life in the war, he was most liberal with the accounts of Indian savagery, and Indian treachery, as he had seen it developed under the fostering care of British influence. And as he had often said he would during the war, he now taught his children to hate the unfortunate race.

CHAPTER VII.

ARLY in the spring the Fosters began
preparations for emigrating to New York
State. Their possessions were reduced as much
as possible, to facilitate traveling, which in those
primitive times, was no small undertaking.

Their goods, together with their stock was
sold at public auction, which was a great event
for the town then, as it is still in many of our
rural hamlets. All of the farming tools and implements, save a few hand tools, were also disposed of at auction. But as in those days more
than one plow was seldom found on a single
farm, and the harrowing was done with brush,
the hay and grain harvested with "arm strong"
mowers and reapers (scythe and cradles), there
were not many implements to sell. Still the auction was a lively affair. Elisha and Nat were the
envy of the other boys of the town, as they beheld them with their father bustling about the
place, getting things ready, and leading up the
stock for the bawling auctioneer to show his wit
and exercise his lungs over. All of the guns,
traps and snares that the boys had accumulated

were retained. For they did not propose to go into the new country unprepared for following the chase, even though they might be handicapped for farming.

Mrs. Foster, woman-like, had planned and arranged to take along enough of her household goods to load two or three carts, but her proceedings were vetoed by the men; and her stock, too, was reduced materially by placing such things as were not absolutely necessary, under the auctioneer's hammer; and although she demurred at first, she afterwards expressed herself as satisfied, when she found they had spared her tools for spinning and working up flax and wool.

At last the final day arrived. Yoking the oxen (which had been retained) to the lumbering two-wheeled cart, they loaded their few possessions, found seats for the women and children, tied their one remaining cow to the rear end of the box and were ready.

To Nat had been assigned the honor of acting as driver of the ox team at the start. Proudly flourishing his whip, he gave the command to "gee up;" the patient, slow-moving oxen leaned forward in their yokes, stepped deliberately off, and the journey to the Mohawk Valley and Adirondack Mountains was begun.

Probably Mrs. Foster alone, of all the family, felt, with any keenness, the pangs of regret at leaving the familiar place of such long and tender associations. If the rest experienced any emotions, they did not pause in their eagerness of anticipation, to entertain them. But to the mother it had been a home of many tender experiences; and stirring events, too, which left their impression on her retentive heart. There at the home they were leaving, all of her children had been born and reared, amid the sturdy struggles of a pioneer life, intensified by the heavy cloud of war which had hung particularly heavy over her home. Hence it was that with a sigh and genuine pang of silent distress, she turned in her seat in the cart, and took a last, lingering and farewell look at the dear old "home" on that bright spring morn.

The children felt no uneasiness, nor experienced any regrets at leaving the familiar surroundings. To them the move was a novelty which contained enough of the romantic to render starting the all-absorbing feature of their young lives at that particular moment. They had no very serious thoughts or concerns for the future; while the past did not, as yet, present the tender and sentimental features it would in after years.

Mr. Foster was indifferent. He had roamed about too much during the last few years of his life to be moved to any feelings of emotion at changing his place of abode.

So it was that the mother alone of all the party possessed those serious thoughts and reveries, which come from such an event as was now happening. But her sigh of regret escaped unnoticed; and soon the joyful laughter of the children and the jovial conversation of the older boys and Mr. Foster cheered her naturally happy soul.

They journeyed by easy stages, camping by the roadside at night; a comfortable shelter of skins was rigged over the box of the cart for the women and children to repose under, while Elisha, Nat and Mr. Foster slept in fur robes on the ground under the shelter of the cart. The cow, which from its position behind the cart, necessarily followed with patience the slow moving vehicle day after day, supplied them with milk to accompany their simple repasts of corn bread, boiled venison or bear meat and roasted potatoes; all prepared by the camp fire.

Their route, necessarily, lay through a partially wild and at best but sparsely settled country. At night, their sleep was often disturbed by the howling wolf, or screaming panther, or by the worrying cattle, tugging at their fastenings, as their keen senses detected danger. When the danger was considered very great, one of the older boys or Mr. Foster would keep watch. The latter often spoke of Indians, and expressed surprise that the "red devils," as he called them, had not put in an appearance. But most of the Indians, at the close of the war of the Revolution, had withdrawn from New England and New York to Canada, and only an occasional band of hunters were to be seen. Nothing was seen of them by the Foster family until they reached the Hudson river.

They arrived at that noble stream just north of where the village of Lansingburg is now situated. All other streams they had encountered they were able to ford. But to cross here at that time, they were obliged to make a raft and ferry themselves and their possessions across. The construction of this raft consumed several days. And as they were engaged in falling timber for the making of it, they observed that they were being watched by some persons on the opposite shore. Who it was they could not imagine. There were no settlers who would care about their cutting trees, and the noble red man, if it was he, did not care for the timber. But that the watchers were Indians, and that they were watching him and his sons with no good intentions, Mr. Foster felt certain.

At last they were ready to trust themselves to their rudely constructed raft, and cross to the "land of promise," which, if not actually "flowing with milk and honey," was at least rich in the opportunities it would afford the family to develope, each in the direction of his individual tastes and likings.

They began early in the day to put their effects on the raft, but it was a slow and tedious task. The cart had been taken apart and carried on in sections, for when they attempted to wheel it on, it had stuck fast in the soft mud of the shore. Then followed the work of getting the cattle onto the floating crib; all was duly accomplished, however, and late in the afternoon they launched out upon the stream, which, at that time of the year, was high and turbulent. After two hours hard work in fighting the swift current, which carried them a mile down the stream, they at last brought their crazy craft safely to the opposite shore and moored it close to the bank, in a little bay. By that time the sun was nearly down.

As they swung their raft in by the shore, and here making it fast to near-by trees, Mr. Foster's quick eye detected an Indian watching their movements from behind a distant tree. It took him but a moment to discover two more skulking warriors behind different trees, watching them intently; and his suspicions of the last two days were confirmed. He said nothing to the rest, however, about the presence of the Indians, but hurried the work of landing. Everything was transferred to the shore, the cart set up, the camp made and supper cooked before dark. Then having gathered his family together, he told them of the Indians he had seen, and apprised them of his fears of an attack from them that night. It was decided that the boys and Mr. Foster should take turns in keeping watch, so that all would be guarded against surprise. Commending them all to the protection of Almighty God, the father told them to go to sleep, while he kept watch until midnight, as he calculated that, if an attack was to be made, it would be before that hour.

He kept his weary and lonely vigil until long after midnight, and then, having heard nothing, he concluded that the real danger was past, and turned the watch over to the boys.

With yawns and expressions of disgust at being roused from their sound slumbers, Nat and Elisha got up and took their father's place; while he crept into the warm place they had vacated. The air was chilly, and the night as black as ink. Seeking one of the cart wheels, the boys spread a wolf robe on the ground, and seating themselves upon it, with their backs supported by the upright wheel, prepared to watch the night out.

As we might have suspected, Elisha had the old smoth bore by his side, and Nat, with characteristic caution, sat with his rifle across his knees, his keen eyes gazing into the darkness and his quick ear strained to catch the least suspicious sound.

Their teeth soon commenced to chatter from the cold, and Elisha declared that he must be allowed to roll himself in the wolf robe on which they were seated, or he would certainly freeze to death. So Nat obligingly arose and paced up and down the camp, while the easy-going Elisha wrapped himself in the wolf robe, and, naturally enough, was soon sound asleep.

But no thought of giving away to sleep entered the mind of Nat. Grasping with firmer grip the stock of his rifle, he paced his little beat with careful step, like an old soldier on guard. It was a trying place for a lad of sixteen, even if he had been brought up in the pioneer life. No sound broke the oppressive stillness. Not even a cricket's chirrup or an owl's hoot dis-

turbed the silence that prevailed. It would have
been a relief to hear a wolf howl, or even a panther scream. For an hour Nat thus kept pacing
his beat, straining every nerve to catch any
possible sign of an approaching foe.

Suddenly the stillness was broken by the sharp
sound of a snapping twig. He stopped as suddenly, and remained as motionless as if frozen
to the ground; but not from fear or fright. For
full three minutes he waited and listened with
all his powers, but not another sound did he
hear, all was as still as before. Yet he knew
that the twig was broken by some approaching
man or beast; which he could not tell.

Finally he detected a very slight rustling in
the bushes a few yards from the camp. He
recognized at once the movements of a man or
men approaching with great caution through the
underbrush. Without stopping to rouse his
father or brother, he raised his rifle and fired
into the bushes, in the direction from whence
the sound came; and springing to the side of the
slumbering Elisha, he snatched up the smooth
bore and sent its contents into the bushes before
that drowsy youth was fairly awake.

Instantly all was commotion in the little
camp. The cattle snorted and struggled at their
fastenings, while the women cried out in alarm,

and little Sybil, in the distress of being thus rudely awakened, and also fear of the darkness, commenced to cry. Elisha sat up, and mildly asked in a hoarse whisper what was the matter. Mr. Foster sprang to the side of his brave son, and asked if it was "Injuns." In a brief and hurried whisper, Nat explained to his father what he had heard in the bushes, and together, with cocked rifles, they waited for more manifestations of the lurking foe. But farther than a great trampling and a snapping and cracking of the twigs and bushes, immediately after Nat fired his charges, they heard nothing. Whether the foe was still concealed in the underbrush, only waiting for them to relax their vigilance before advancing, or whether he was killed, or had retreated, they were unable to even guess.

The remainder of the night was spent with the combined watchings of Mr. Foster and Nat, and even Elisha, who had been somewhat frightened and thoroughly awakened by his brother's rapid shots, now found no difficulty in keeping awake. The few remaining hours of the night passed without incident. And as the gray dawn began to manifest itself, they breathed easier, waiting until broad daylight, however, before they ventured to stir about or rouse the rest of the family. Upon going a few yards into the bushes, they found them trampled and broken. Along the trail, which had evidently been made by their nocturnal visitors in their retreat, there was a stream of blood, deeply dyeing the leaves and bushes, as far as they followed it. It gave unmistakable evidence that at least one of the party, if not more, had been shot and borne away by companions. One or both of Nat's shots had told. He had drawn his first blood from an Indian, if indeed he had not killed the warrior, for the blood-bespattered leaves and gory trail told plainly that it was the life blood of the wounded savage that was being shed.

"I reckon, Nat," said Mr. Foster, as he examined the bloody trail, "that you made the daylight shine through one or two of the red devils."

"But how could that be, dad: said the skeptical Elisha, "Nat shot 'em in the dark."

"Humph," said Mr. Foster, contemptuously "the daylight is a shinen through 'em by this time anyhow, if that gore speaks for anything. I don't think this is a very healthy place for us to be a sojourning in so very long either," he continued, "the critters might come back and get revenge on us. We'd better be gettin' out."

So a hasty breakfast was cooked and eaten and the cattle brought from their browsing in the woods before they had half finished their morning's feed. And before the sun had begun to climb the heavens, they left the place.

In crossing the Hudson, the Fosters had finished the hardest part of their journey. They were now entering the famous valley in which they intended to settle. Mr. Foster had determined upon no particular place for their location, but as they journeyed on towards the valley they received wonderful accounts from the settlers along their route, of the village of Johnstown, which had been settled before the war by Sir William Johnson. As Mr. Foster had also heard something of it while in these parts early in the war, he resolved to settle in that locality. Although it was not in the valley where he had at first intended to locate, he decided that Johnstown and its vicinity, being advantageous for hunting and fishing, as well as farming, would be better than the valley. So turning their course to the northwest, they pushed on until they came to the famous fish house built by Sir William, and here they decided to settle.

Again Mr. Foster erected a little cabin of logs, for his new home, although it was not destined to serve as long as the one he had built so many years before in New Hampshire. Having the sturdy strength of his two oldest sons to assist

9

him this time, and that of his neighbors as well, the cabin was built in a much shorter time.

A wonderfully fraternal spirit prevailed among the settlers of those early times, and it was particularly predominant about Johnstown. Sir William himself set the example in its early days, when he founded the town, and the settlers imbibed the spirit. So that whenever a new family came to those parts to build a home, a "bee" was always inaugurated and a "log rolling" was had and a good serviceable cabin was built in a few days. With some further details, in the way of closing the chinks between the logs, the construction of a fireplace and chimney, and the hanging of the door, the house was all ready for occupancy. In rare cases, I have heard of such little matters as building a chimney and hanging a door being omitted entirely, smoke escaping through a hole in the roof and a deer's hide or other skin, covering the opening in the wall, which answered for a door. Of course these are exceptional instances, and settlers who were obliged to forego such necessary things as chimneys and doors must have been in very straitened circumstances. The new cabin of the Fosters, I am told, was comfortably finished, with one room on the ground, and a sleeping place above, under the roof. It also had a chimney and door.

"Such log cabins * * * were the houses of most of our forefathers."

Such log cabins, with their two simple apartments, were the homes of most of our forefathers. In such humble homes many of the present Americans' immediate ancestors were born and reared. The families were nearly always large, many including members who have become prominent in our country's history.

The Fosters had lived in their new home less than two months ere destruction came to it from the hand of the savage Indian, together with the capture of Zilpha. It happened one afternoon when all the family, excepting Zilpha and Nat, were away to a bee being held for the benefit of another new family just arrived in the neighborhood. The Indians probably knowing this, undoubtedly laid their plans accordingly, and raided the Foster dwelling when they expected to find no one but women or children about. Early in the afternoon Zilpha was engaged in washing the dishes after the noonday meal of herself and brother. Her work was on a bench under the shade of a tree just outside the cabin. Nat was inside engaged in cleaning some traps.

After lurking about in the bushes at the edge of the woods and seeing no one about but the girl, the Indians stealthily made their way towards the cabin, and coming up behind the unsuspecting maiden, who was blithely humming a little air, they seized and gagged her before she could make a single outcry of alarm. The sudden cessation of her singing, however, attracted Nat's attention, and peering out of the cabin door, he was horrified to see his sister in the clutches of the red men. It took the lad but an instant to take in the situation. His first impulse was to rush out, or open fire from the cabin, and attempt to slay single handed all of his sister's captors. And no doubt, if here had been a rifle in the cabin, he would have rashly undertaken it. But the only fire-arm there was the old smoth bore, and even that old piece, though it had often done him and his brother good service in emergencies, would not do to wipe out the ten or more Indians in the party.

Here, Nat's quick perception of an awkward situation and the very best mode of action, which he ever afterwards manifested, was shown. The party was too strong for him to hope in any way to overcome single-handed. His only hope was in remaining undiscovered and, watching his chance, escape and warn the settlers at the bee. All this flashed through his mind in an instant, and as he saw the Indians turn and come towards the cabin, he put it in action. At his feet was a trap door leading into a simple hole, dug under the cabin floor to serve as a cellar.

Lifting the door, he dropped into the hole and noiselessly closed it after him, just as the Indian in the lead stepped upon the threshhold. Then followed a half hour of agony and suspense. The Indians ransacked the cabin and searched even the loft, talking constantly in their own language. Every moment he feared they would notice the trap door and, investigating the hole underneath, discover him. But it escaped their observation.

The pleadings of his sister, as they ungagged her, beseeching them to let her go, nearly drove him frantic, and he could hardly restrain himself from leaping forth from his hiding place and throwing himself upon the Indians in a wild attempt to deliver her. But he restrained himself and remained silent. He hardly dared to breathe as the Indians trampled over his head and paused at the trap door as if to lift it. At last they departed, taking the weeping girl with them. Nat cautiously lifted the door a trifle and looked out. The coast was clear, and he crawled up, very weak and shaky from his cramped position and restrained excitement. As he expected, he found that the Indians had fired the cabin before taking their departure, having started the fire in the loft, under the roof. It was a roaring furnace before he dared leave.

He watched the Indians as they crossed the clearing and made for the woods. At last they disappeared in the foliage, and then, with a bound, he was out of the doomed cabin and speeding away like a deer to warn the settlers. He ran with terrific speed the whole of the two miles, and was so winded when he arrived that he could hardly speak. But he managed to gasp out—"Indians," "Cabin afire," and "Zilpha." The settlers instantly guessed the whole affair and the men began hastily to prepare for pursuit. As but few of the men had brought their guns (danger from the Indians being regarded as over) some little time was consumed in sending fleet boys to the various homes after these very necessary weapons.

Mr. Foster and Elisha had brought their rifles, thinking they might have an opportunity to shoot some game, and the old man could hardly be restrained from starting off alone in pursuit of the Indians.

In a quarter of an hour's time all were ready. Nat had sufficiently recovered his wind to head the party, and borrowing a gun started off again on a dog trot, which he kept up, setting the pace for the party until they arrived at the site of the Foster home. Nothing was left of the cabin but a smouldering heap of ashes. As they came in sight of it, young Nat's passions rose.

"Here," he exclaimed, "is my life's work. I'll hate the red devils worse'n dad, and I'll shoot 'em every chance I git."

This passionate expression arose from the thought of his beautiful sister in the possession of the dusky red men. Although during his life he shot many Indians, yet he never seemed to harbor a particularly bitter feeling against them, nor made shooting them his life's work. No doubt this and other experiences, together with his father's instructions upon the subject, made him quite undervalue the life of an American Indian, and caused him to shoot them without hesitation, whenever they threatened his life or trespassed upon his rights. But for a ferocious and blood-thirsty character, we will have to look elsewhere; for, as I will endeavor to show in following his life, he was possessed of a naturally kind disposition. He was liberal, even to the Indians, against whom he was now swearing eternal vengeance.

The pursuing party paused but a moment at the site of the devastated home, and then Nat led the way to the place where the Indians had entered the woods. He took the lead himself, and assumed the responsibility of detecting and following their trail. At that early age the lad had already gained a reputation for keenness in following trails of deer, moose and other game. And now, as he set out for the first time on a genuine Indian's trail, his hunter's instinct was quickened by love for his sister, and hatred for her dusky captors. So there was nothing strange in his taking the lead over older and more experienced men in the party, and unhesitatingly and unerringly following the faint and half blind trail, over hills, across streams and through marshes. The Indians had taken pains to cover their trail as much as possible, but they could not conceal it from the eagle eye of that lad whose instinct was sharpened by affection, and whose heart throbbed with a brother's love, while it also beat with hatred for their cowardly, detestable conduct.

All the afternoon they followed the trail over the hills and through glens. At first they thought the Indians were carrying Zilpha, for no imprint of a shoe could be found on the trail. But after they had gone several miles, and had come to a little stream where they stopped to drink, one of the party found her shoes concealed in the ledge of a rock. Then they knew that the brutal savages were compelling her to walk with unprotected feet in order that she might not leave any mark of her leather shoes. Their belief in this theory was confirmed, as some miles farther on, they found blood stains plainly made by footprints, on some rocks the Indians had gone over. They undoubtedly came from the bruised and bleeding feet of the fair Zilpha. Twice they found pieces of the homespun dress she wore clinging to the bushes.

As the afternoon advanced, they observed that the trail was growing fresher, and they had good hopes of overtaking and surprising the Indians. Nat finally proposed that they stop and let him climb a tree to see if he could discover any signs of their camp fire. To this proposition they all agreed, and pausing, they watched Nat as he made his way to a little knoll in which stood a tall birch tree. He ascended as readily, if not as rapidly as a squirrel.

His position at the top commanded a fine view of the surrounding country. To the south lay the uneven land over which they had come, and to the north was a gentle valley, through which there evidently flowed a small creek. Beyond the valley stretched the broken and hazy mountains, the refuge of the Indians. The trees of the forest presented, in every direction, an unbroken bank of green foliage. From the center of the valley, less than two miles away, Nat observed a thin circle of smoke ascending from the tree tops, evidently coming from a very small fire. It was so faint that an unpracticed eye would not have noticed it. It undoubtedly marked the location of the Indians' camp, who were evidently preparing their supper from a very small fire, in order to make as little smoke as possible.

Sliding down from his perch, Nat reported his observations and his opinion, to which they all agreed. The best mode of advancing upon the Indians was then discussed. It was thought that the Indians, fearing pursuit, would not stop long at their present location, but would push on as soon as they had eaten their supper in order to reach the mountains. So it was decided to advance at once to within a quarter of a mile of their camp and then send scouts forward to reconnoiter. If they saw that the Indians were making no preparations for remaining during the night, they would attack them at once. But if, on the contrary, there was evidence of their remaining, they would wait until it was dark and the Indians asleep, when the chances of success would be greater.

They accordingly went carefully forward until they came to what they judged was a quarter of a mile from the creek where the Indians' camp must be, then they stopped and Nat and his father went forward to look over the ground.

They came up, in the underbrush, to the very edge of the bubbling brook, with the Indians' camp directly opposite them, on the other bank. The warriors were seated on the ground before a tiny fire of sticks, eating some broiled venison and parched corn. Zilpha was bound to a tree a short distance away, but where the Indians could watch her.

Father and son embraced each other as they beheld the girl still alive, though she was in a pitiable condition. Her hair was disheveled, and her dress in tatters, while her stockings had been completely worn out and torn off by the rocks and bushes. Her feet were cut and bleeding.

How to get Zilpha out of the clutches of these fiends was the question. If they were to surprise them without success, the first thing her captors would do would be to kill her. Strategy alone would be successful.

The Indians were making no preparations for the night, evidently intending to start on their journey again as soon as they had finished their meal. So what was to be done must be done quickly. Here it was that the experience Mr. Foster had had in the war came to his aid.

The Indians' fire was in an opening in the woods and brush, a few yards from the bank of the creek flowing from west to east. The Indians themselves were seated in a semi-circle around the fire, facing the stream, their backs to the north. Zilpha was bound to a tree by the bank of the stream at their left. The old soldier immediately resolved to send a detachment of his party around to the west of the camp and have them come up and fire upon the Indians from the northwest, and on their rear. At the first volley the Indians, not disabled, would immediately seize their rifles and turn to open fire on the attacking party, thus giving the party on the south an opportunity to sally forth, discharge their pieces, and recover the girl. An exceedingly good bit of generalship on a small scale. Mr. Foster repeated these plans to Nat and then dispatched his boy to the waiting ones. He gave Nat the responsibility of leading the flanking party, while he was to send Elisha with the others to him.

Nat hastened away and the old man was left alone. Only for a few moments, however, as he was quickly joined by the men Nat had sent him. Together they waited in silence, communicating only by signs or whispers, ready to spring from their hiding place as soon as Nat's party engaged the Indians' attention from the rear. In a short time Mr. Foster's eye, though dimmed, caught the gleam of the polished barrel of a rifle

in the hands of one of the flanking party in the
bushes away to the rear of the unsuspecting Indians. The latter, by this time, had finished
eating and were already beginning to tighten up
their belts preparatory to resuming their journey.

Signalling to his companions, Mr. Foster
cocked his rifle and all prepared to spring from
their covert. Suddenly a sheet of flame shot out
from the bushes behind the seated Indians, and
the reports of six rifles rang upon the air. Four
of the Indians never rose from the ground.
Those who were left alive sprang to their feet
with rifles poised; but before they could fire,
Mr. Foster and his men were out of the thicket
with a yell, discharging their pieces at the Indians as they rushed towards the bound and now
struggling girl. This volley left but five of the
Indians alive, and as Nat and his party rushed
into view with a whoop and a yell, they turned
and ran into the brush.

The father and brothers rushed simultaneously
towards Zilpha. Mr. Foster was so overjoyed
that he could only fall on his daughter's neck
and weep. But Nat quickly cut the thongs which
bound her, and tenderly kissing her, said: "You
see, sis, I didn't sneak into that hole for nothing,
did I?"

Night was coming on and the party must

make haste back to the settlements. Gathering up the rifles and implements of the dead Indians, they started. They had brought the shoes of the captive, and, after bathing her feet, she put them on and stood the long tramp to the settlement very well. They reached it long after dark, but found all the settlers waiting anxiously for them; and great was the rejoicing at the return of the fair Zilpha, who, for her grace of manners and beauty of countenance, was already a favorite in the settlement.

The Foster home was soon rebuilt, and as before, on the edge of the forests. Not even this serious occurrence could scare the hardy old soldier or his brave family away. They were never again molested by the Indians, but their days spent in peace and prosperity.

The only other melancholy feature of this raid by the Indians was the destruction of the very famous old smooth bore rifle. Elisha particularly mourned its loss; to him it had been a constant companion, and for whom it had frequently done invaluable service in delivering him from great personal danger at the last extremity. The old fowling piece, as I have mentioned, was the only firearm in the cabin at the time the Indians made their raid, and they had either overlooked it, or did not consider it worth carrying away. Only its warped and twisted barrel was found in the ashes of the home. Thus lamentably ended the career of the famous old gun, which had figured so conspicuously in the early history of the boys.

The residence of the Foster family at Johnstown marked the development of the boys and girls into men and women, and the addition of four children to the household. The following children were born after the family settled at Johnstown, or more properly the Fish House. Elihu in 1784, Polly in 1788, Lydia in 1791, and Shubal in 1795. The last named son afterwards figured in several adventures with his brother Nat. Zilpha's hand was won by a gallant swain of the neighborhood, and Elisha's heart was smitten by a fair daughter of the settlement. Her he married.

This "stepping off" of his brother made Nat feel rather blue at first. But as their hunting and trapping excursions were to be continued as before, he expressed himself as satisfied.

Thus was Nat matured under the sturdy discipline, yet free life of a hunter and trapper. He seldom allowed a month to go by without taking his gun and dog and going for a tramp of two or three days in the wilderness in pursuit of game. Farming was always irksome to him, though he never neglected to help his father with the farm work, particularly during seed time and harvest. He never neglected his own farm when he came to possess one. But as soon as fall and winter approached he would bring forth his traps and snares, and rubbing off the coat of tallow that had been put on in the spring to keep them from rusting, he laid out and carried on his work for the winter. Many and varied were his experiences during the years spent under the paternal roof at Johnstown.

But realizing that I must omit many details of his interesting life, let me pass on to the time when he reached man's estate.

CHAPTER VIII.

NAT was a large muscular fellow when he attained his majority. He possessed the peculiarity of having double or molar teeth all around his jaws; and being double jointed, with other peculiarities, which gave him great strength. His early life had been, as we have seen, one of hardships, with frequent encounters with ferocious wild animals and a number of encounters with the still wild Indian. All of this, coupled with the entire absence of education, (which it was impossible for him to get when a lad) made him adapted to a life of daring adventure and exciting exploits that would test the nerve and muscle of a man.

He once said of himself that when he was twenty-one he was ready to measure his strength with any man, no matter what color, "whether white, black or red." He had inherited his father's huge frame; this, with his vigorous toil in the fields, extensive tramps in the woods when growing, together with the muscular peculiarity noted, made him at this time the possessor of unusual strength and endurance, and endowed him with dauntless courage, almost bordering on recklessness. Foster has given an interesting account of an adventure which occurred in his twenty-first year and has been preserved by the family tradition, and which I will give in presumably his own words.

"It was in the month of August," he was wont to say, "and work on father s farm being slack, and I twenty-one, thought it time to begin to think of striking out for myself. So I went on a tramp north, deep in the woods, for the purpose of selecting a route for hunting and trapping in the fall and winter. I filled my pack basket with provisions and with my rifle and my faithful bitch dog Rose by my side, who could scent any kind of a varmit a mile away. I started off. I soon found I could kill and secure all the game I wished, but it wasn't late enough in the season for prime fur. I tramped into the great wilderness as far as Piesco Lake, where I proposed to make my camp for the fall and winter's hunt. After constructing a log camp on the shore of the lake, which took me a couple of days, I started back for home on the morning of the third day, intending to reach there by the following night. I tramped leisurely along in the forenoon, stopping to note favorable streams and

places to locate my traps during the coming season. I stopped for a considerable of a spell at
Sacandaga river and its vicinity, and it was the
middle of the afternoon before I thought of
starting off homeward in real earnest. Finally
I started off, walking merrily along, congratu-
lating myself on the pleasantness of the trip.
No Indians to bother me and lots of game,
though not prime. I only killed one deer and
that was to get its saddle, to add fresh meat to
my larder

"As I was thus engaged in these pleasant
reveries, my dog suddenly commenced to growl,
while every hair on her back pointed straight
towards her head. I asked her if there was any
game around and she only growled the more.
Then I asked her if it was Injuns, and she came
close up to me and looked up to my face as
much as to say yes. So I sat down on a log
among some bushes and listened. I couldn't see
or hear a thing, yet I knew from my dog's action that some kind of varmints was around,
and from her actions I suspected it was Injuns.
I waited and listened, I guess, fifteen minutes
before I heard anything. Then I heard the
footsteps of someone approaching. My faithful dog at my command ceased growling, but
crowded close to me, all the while on nettles,
and shaking from excitement.

"I was situated on the top of a small knoll, just above the river. The noise of the approaching footsteps came along the bank of the river from the west on the same side I was on. In a few minutes I saw three Indians coming up the bank of the river. But I kept perfectly still, and thought I would let the red devils pass. I quickly noted that there was only one gun in the party and I could easily have cleaned out the three of them by first picking off the one that carried the gun. But I thought if they behaved themselves I would not molest them, though I ached to crack 'em, for I had particularly hated the race ever sence they captured Zilpha. But I didn't know as these particular three had ever done me or my folks any harm, so I let them alone. They passed by the foot of the knoll where me and my dog were concealed, and proceeding on down the stream a few rods, they commenced to build a fire and make a camp. After watching them a little while I commenced to think of slipping off, when to my surprise, I saw two more of the red devils coming down the river bank. They walked in Indian file, and as they passed me, I was dumfounded to see a white child apparently eight or nine years old, walking between them. It was tired out, and as it lagged, the Indian behind it would strike it with the handle of his hatchet. I couldn't tell at first whether it was a boy or girl, with its clothes torn off, but from its long hair I calculated it was a little girl.

"You can imagine my feelings. I instantly thought of my sister whom I had assisted in rescuing from the Indians five years before. And here was some one else's sister, of far more tender years than was mine, at the mercy of these savage brutes. I immediately determined to get the girl out of their clutches or die in the attempt. I noted that the red devil in the lead carried a gun. My first impulse was to shoot him on the spot. But I instantly recollected that the one in the rear would sink his tomahawk into the head of the child the moment I fired, so I kept still. They came up to the camp and the child, although nearly helpless from fatigue, was bound to a tree. Then all five of the red skins went on building their camp, cutting boughs and gathering firewood. As it grew dark their fire was replenished, and as it burned up it lighted up the whole of the camp. I saw the villains very plainly as they lounged on their boughs eating their venison, giving a few morsels to the child, but making no offers to release the poor thing from her strained position.

"All the while I was setting my wits to work how to get the child. I knew very well that I had an all night's job on my hands. But to get possession of the captive, I resolved to do or die. I was thirty miles from home, from any settlement, in fact; and nothing around me but wild beasts and this band of red savages.

"The first thing I did after it got quite dark, was to carry my pack basket about a mile down the trail towards home. There I left it and my dog to guard it and returned to my former position on the hill. This took me probably half an hour. When I got back I saw by the light of the fire that the Injuns had rolled themselves in their blankets. I waited for an hour, until the fire had burnt very low and I judged the Injuns were asleep. Then I commenced to work up towards their camp, using the utmost caution, for an Injun always sleeps with one eye open. But in spite of my care, when I had got up close to their camp, and was settling down to take further observations, a stick I had unwittingly placed my foot on snapped with a loud report. In an instant all five of them Injuns were on their feet and yelling as only their kind of the human race can, as they give their whoop of surprise or alarm. But I was not the only creature prowling about their camp, and taking

observations, for the whoop of the red devils, as they sprang to their feet and seized their guns and hatchets, startled a huge panther that was in a tree right over their heads. He, too, it seems, had been sneaking up to the camp, only he had been more successful than I had been in approaching without disturbing the slumbering savages. As the Injuns yelled the beast gave an awful scream and sprang into the bushes on the opposite side of the camp to me, and all five of the red skins rushed pell mell into the bushes after him, supposing he was the one that had disturbed them. This mistake was my opportunity. As they plunged into the darkness, I rushed forward and quickly cutting the thongs which bound the little girl, took her into my arms and told her not to cry and I would take her back to her folks, and hurried away. Providence had been kind and provided a way which was very wonderful to me, to get the child without any struggle with her captors. With these thoughts in my mind I carried her to my basket and dog, sooner than any Injun could have gone without any load to carry. I set the child down by the basket and listened, but could hear nothing. But still I knew this was a race for life. I knew the red devils would return to their camp in a very few moments

after leaving it, for if they did not shoot the panther right away they would let it go. I had
heard no gun, so I knew that by this time they
had returned and found their captive gone.
Probably they were already on my trail.

"My pack basket was a good-sized one and I
decided to carry the child in that. Throwing
out everything but my blanket, I arranged that
in the shape of a seat. Then I put the child in
the basket and strapped it on my back and telling the poor thing to stop crying, (for she was
weeping in a quiet sort of way), and go to sleep,
if she could, I started off for civilization, picking
my way as best I could and covering up my
trail as much as possible. How soon the red
devils would be upon me I did not know, but I
relied on my dog to tell me. By daylight I
judged I had covered some six or eight miles.
I entered a gap or small valley between two
hills as the sun commenced to rise. I began to
think by this time that a few moments rest and
a bite of breakfast would give me strength, for
the Injuns had cheated me out of my supper
the night before. So I concluded to go up one
of those little ravines, washed out by water rush-
ing down a hill in the spring, for I could conceal
my trail better on the pebbles and stones. So I
made my way up one of the gorges about twenty

rods and set down my basket and helped the girl
from her cramped position. I had only reserved
a piece of bread and a bit of cold venison from
the provisions I threw away, and about half a
pint of rum in a pocket flask. Dividing the
meat between the dog and the child, I munched
the bread and drank some of the spirits and felt
much refreshed.

"As we ate our breakfast I questioned the
girl, and found that her name was Mary French
and that she was ten years old, but she was small
for her age. Her home, she said, was near
Johnstown. And that she with several children
had gone into the woods the day before to
gather blackberries, and while she was separated from the others the Indians had suddenly
appeared and carried her off before she could
give any alarm. This accounted for the leisurely
manner the Indians had journeyed. For the
little one being secretly captured, her people
would think her lost, and so would not be so apt
to discover their trail and follow them.

"As I was thinking of starting on again, my
dog commenced to growl and tremble with excitement. I knew that the red devils were at last
on my track and very near me. I knew, too, if
there was going to be a fight, my position was
a good one. But I decided to keep still and let

them pass if they would, for with the child on my hands, I did not want to commence a fight five to one. And, too, I knew that the child's people must soon be on the Indians' trail, if they were any kind of hunters at all, and must be that way before long.

"Soon two of the Injuns went past on a dog trot. One had a gun and the other his knife and hatchet. I let them, pass for I very well knew that if I commenced the fight they would soon know that I was alone, and if I didn't succeed in wiping them all out at once, they would lay by and wait for me to give up, if it took them a week. In a few minutes the other three hove in sight, going at the same pace as the others. They were looking at the ground, trying to follow my trail, but it was a hard one to follow. They did not discover it leading into the gulch where I was, but passed on. I don't know how far they went, but in a few moments they came back, looking for my trail. They finally found it at the foot of the hill, and started up the gorge where I was. I concluded that now was the time for action. The little one commenced to cry at the sight of the dreadful fiends coming up the ravine, but I hushed her up and told her to keep still, and I would send them back to Canada, which I did, as you shall see.

"The red skins, intent on studying my footprints among the loose pebbles, were half way up the gulch before I made a move. They were in single file, the first one carrying the gun. Now I cocked my rifle and thought I would see what a shot would do in the way of 'scaring' them off. I fired, and the leader dropped his firearm. The other two stood still a minute to locate my position, I suppose, and I quickly loaded and fired again. With that the red devil last in the line turned and ran for all he was worth towards Piesco Lake; and I hastily loaded and fired again in his direction, just to help him along; but I did not follow him. Like enough he got there; and maybe they all got back to Canada, but I know they did not come any farther up the gorge. We kept quiet for a while, the child, the dog and myself, but finally we heard a gun fired not more than a quarter of a mile away. Soon another and still another shot was fired, and then I immediately began to prepare to fire return shots, for three shots were the signals in those days, when people were looking for lost children. I fired my three shots and they were answered at once. Then I was sure that some of little Mary's friends were in the vicinity. So putting her in my basket again, I started off, and after more shots and some hallooing we got

together.   Little Mary's father was in the party
and their meeting was a joyful one."

In some such a manner as this Nat was wont
to narrate his adventures in after years to his
grand-children, one of which he was particularly
fond of, and when the lad was six or seven years
old, and he an old man, he would amuse the
child for hours by telling him adventures like
the above.   And by reason of this custom of his,
I am enabled to give so many details of his life,
they being preserved in the memory of his
grand-children.

In spite of this serious brush with the Indians
in the then great wilderness about the Sacandaga River, I am told that the young hunter
went on his contemplated hunting and trapping
excursion to Piesco Lake the following fall, and
spent a most profitable season, the first of many
subsequent ones, hunting and trapping for business and pleasure.   It was in his twenty-first
year that young Nat first met Nicholas Stoner,
another famous hunter and trapper of Northern
New York.   Stoner was a few years older than
Nat, but the young man's straight and sturdy
frame, together with his being partial for hunting, and his manly ways, won at once the admiration and lasting friendship of Stoner.   From
their first meeting they were warm friends, and

often companioned together in tramps and hunts, and other occasions, as the following incident will show. It was the year after Nat's skirmish with the Indians, just narrated, that he consented to pay a visit with Stoner to a village on the Sacandaga River, to participate in some sports and games to be held there on "Independence Day," as the Fourth of July was always called in those days.

Stoner had so much confidence in the superior strength and ability of his new friend that he was sure he would easily carry off all the honors of the day. Young Foster and his companion reached St. Johnsville in the early part of the forenoon of the day of sports, for Independence Day was distinctively a day of sports, as it was never allowed to pass without games of foot racing, jumping and wrestling being on the programme. Nat's appearance with Stoner, who was well known in the village, created no little surprise and interest. The young man, straight as an arrow and over six feet tall, was dressed in a striking costume gotten up by Stoner for the occasion. He wore a heavy hunting shirt, laced with thongs of deerskin. His thighs were covered with a pair of buckskin breeches, supported at the waist by a wide belt of leather, while a pair of leggings and moccasins of buckskin, neatly worked and beaded, covered his feet and legs. This costume was completed by a cocked hat of the times. He was at once the most conspicuous figure of the assembled crowds. The sports were opened with a free-for-all foot race of forty rods; the best six in the race were to run two more heats, and the prize given to the winner in the last heat or run. Nat took his place with the motley crowd that prepared to run the first time. But following the private advice of his friend, he only kept up with the leaders, and apparently was no better than the ordinary when the dash was finished. And in the second run, he only came out a foot ahead of the others. But it was in the third heat that he was to show himself as one of extraordinary speed, though he was already exciting great interest, and many inquiries were made as to who this strange young man, clad in buckskin, was. Stoner would not give his name to any of his friends, and Nat himself, in obedience to Stoner's instructions, would tell no one. He would only say that his name was Leatherstocking, and that he came from a long distance through the woods. A very significant fact which I will show later.

An old gentleman of the village approached him and respectfully asked him his name and where from, but Nat gave him only an evasive

answer, though something in the old man's appearance and manner attracted his attention, and
he thought he had seen him before. But as Nat
had never been in the village before, he concluded it was only a fancy, and forgot all about
it, particularly as the third and last call for the
foot race was now being announced. The six
contestants quickly placed themselves in line.
There was no "fixing up" in those days or strip-
ping and rubbing down if sprinters, for they ran
in their ordinary clothes, discarding their coat
and hat. Stoner, knowing well how this last run
would terminate, resolved to prepare an even
greater surprise for the assembly than would be
afforded by Nat's mere winning the race. So he
found a long pole and going to the end of the
race course, he took up his position there and
placed one end of the pole on his own shoulder,
while he got another man to support it at the
other end, thus making a hurdle five feet in
height. When the word was given to start Nat
gave a bound which placed his competitors in
the rear, and distancing them all, he dashed over
the course and cleared the pole with a mighty
leap, before the other runners had gone over
half the course. Naturally the young stranger
was loudly cheered as he returned to the starting place accompanied by Stoner, and he was

immediately led away to receive the prize, which was a beaded cap made by the young ladies of the village. It was presented to him by a handsome young woman, who modestly but pleasantly asked the victor his name. Nat received the cap with a graceful bow, but as before, declined to give his name, merely answering that he came from a long distance through the woods.

But for all he gave such a quiet answer, his mind was turbulent and confused, for he was certain he had seen the young woman's face before, but where or when he could not imagine; but concealing his confusion as much as possible, he turned and walked away with Stoner.

Nat was not able to hide his excitement from his friend, however, who thought he had been smitten by the fair face of the girl, for he immediately began to tease him by telling him how the girl was smitten too.

"Do you really think she knew me?" asked Nat very innocently.

"Know you," said Stoner, "how could she know you, when you've been in the woods all your life; why she is a daughter of that old fellow that spoke to you after the second heat," he continued, all unconscious of the excitement his announcement was stirring up in the heart of his friend.

But Nat kept his excitement and his own thoughts to himself, and turned the conversation to other subjects. There were a number of other sports to take place, but he no longer had a desire to participate in them, for he could only think of the fair face of the girl whose hands had placed the cap on his head. He took it off repeatedly to examine it, and wondered as he looked at the marvelous needlework, how much of it had been done by her own fingers. In the afternoon the wrestling matches were to take place. There were many calls for the young stranger who wore the leather leggins, and there was a loud hurrah as Nat appeared in the crowd. But still he did not wish to take part in any of the matches, but said he would rather look on. There were two or three bouts between some of the younger lads of the village, and then a big burly fellow, known in the village for his prowess, stepped into the ring and challenged any one in the assembly to engage with him, but no one responded, for the challenger was too well known in the village as a wrestler. He repeated his challenge, and as no one responded, this feature of the day's sports promised to be very tame; until some one suggested that the stranger take hold. But Nat shook his head decisively as the fellow in the ring bawled out: "Yes, bring on the bully and I will meet him."

11

This taunt was too much for Nat, and with his cheeks burning with indignation and his eyes flashing, he stepped forward and asked the conditions of the match. "Collar and elbow, best two in three, you fool," blurted out his antagonist, who was plainly spoiling for a fray. Nat paid no attention to this sally, but pausing at the edge of the ring, spoke up in a clear voice and said: "Gentlemen, there will be no hardness on my part if this man throws me, and if I am lucky enough to throw him he must bear no ill-will towards me, on no other terms will I enter the ring." The eager crowd quickly answered an agreement to this with shouts of "Go on, go on." Nat tightened his belt and handed his prize cap, which he was still wearing, to Stoner, who whispered to his friend to be sure and preserve the honor of the cap; and with a cheery "never fear," Nat stepped into the ring. The man our hero was to meet was about thirty years old; he was six feet and two inches in height, in fact, a perfect giant to behold. Nat in spite of his own height, looked small beside him. To all appearances the old wrestler had the advantage, as he himself probably firmly believed. But Nat was as spry as a cat, and his double joints gave him the strength of two men; but all this was unknown to his antagonist, who was regarded as the best wrestler in all the country. He had no idea that this strange lad, who came from no one knew where, would be anything but a plaything in his hands. But he was soon to be undeceived.

The first remark made by "Sandy," as the fellow was called, was, "Young man, what is your weight?"

"One hundred and eighty pounds, sir," answered Nat, respectfully, "and now, sir," he continued, "you will please to give me your avoirdupois."

"Two hundred and sixteen pounds," promptly answered Sandy. "And why do you ask," he continued, eyeing Nat curiously.

"Oh, I just thought I would know how much I've got to lift, that's all," was Nat's cool reply.

"Young man," said Sandy, "you wont lift that weight to-day; the proof of the pudding is in the eating; come on."

"So you say," retorted Nat, as he approached his opponent.

The sport began; step by step they approached each other and finally got down to real work, when Nat put his foot at his antagonist's knee and Sandy gave a trip and twitch calculated to throw Nat: But he was prepared for this;

the trip did not reach, and Nat landed Sandy flat on his back.

The hurrah that went up from the crowd was deafening.

"Sandy is down, Sandy is down," was the cry. The two hundred and sixteen pounds had been lifted very easily. In a few moments order was restored, and Sandy, anxious to redeem himself, shouted, "Come on, boy, come on, 1 will show you that mistakes will happen to the best of men."

They now engaged in the second match. Nat did not wait for any false moves this time, but showed his great and superior strength by stepping on Sandy's toe and lifting him from the ground, when he threw him on his back again.

By this time Sandy was in a rage. And not satisfied with the result, wanted to try again. But Nat said: "No; twice is enough, for its the best two in three, you know, and I've had that." But still Sandy insisted; but Nat declared it would not be according to the terms, for it would then be "three out of three."

"Oh, don't be so sure, my lad," retorted Sandy, "just come on and I will show you I was only fooling."

"No," answered Nat, "you would not be satisfied, anyhow."

Then Sandy wanted to fight. But at this Nat told him he would probably come out second best as he had already done. With that Sandy called Nat a coward, and such other hard names, that it required his best efforts to keep cool.

At last Sandy said if Nat would take only one "back hold" with him he would be satisfied. Now this was Nat's favorite hold, so he immediately told Sandy that if that would satisfy him, he would consent. In less than a minute the two contestants were together. Sandy, no doubt, thought he was the strongest of the two, and if he had gotten Nat down he probably intended to punish him to his satisfaction before the crowd interfered. But such was not the case, for Nat's peculiar build enabled him to settle the affair very quickly. He approached Sandy, gave "fond embrace" for about a quarter of a minute, and then let go, when Sandy fell to the ground in a heap, bleeding from the nose.

This settled the wrestling. Nat was at once the hero of the day, and the crowd, cheering loudly, were preparing to carry him triumphantly to the tavern, when a great commotion was observed in another crowd of the villagers on the river bank, and the cry reached them of "a man and woman in the water." Hearing this, Nat sprang from the shoulders of the men and ran as only he could, to the river. There he saw a boat bottom side up, and two persons, a man and a woman, struggling in the water. The man was just able to keep his head above the surface and struggle weakly towards the bank, while the woman was being swept away by the current. She sank as he was looking, and as she appeared again, Nat recognized the face of the young woman who had excited his interest in the morning; and as she sank for the third time, he plunged into the stream and reached her, only by diving and groping for her on the muddy bottom of the river. He made his way to the bank with the girl in his arms, and tenderly assisted in carrying her to a house. He knew who she was now. From two little telltale moles on her neck he was convinced that it was none other than Mary Wilson, the friend and sweetheart of his childhood; and the old gentleman who had spoken to him in the morning, who had been rescued by others from the river, was her father, who had on one occasion so ill-treated him when he was a lad. As soon as he learned that their name was Wilson, thus knowing that his convictions were true, he started for home, in spite of the protestations of his friend Stoner.

As soon as Mr. Wilson recovered from his ducking he sent for the stranger and hero of the day to reward him for his crowning act of gallantry and bravery, but of course, he was nowhere to be found.

Months afterward, he learned who Nat was, and sent a message to him, telling him he remembered with regret his treatment of him at one time in his boyhood, and offering him any reward he might ask for the service he had rendered him in saving his only daughter. It is said Nat sent back word that he was welcome to the service he had rendered, but that the treatment he had received at his hands could never be forgotten.

Foster was once asked later in his life why he did not claim the girl as a reward, and he said he could not marry the daughter of a Tory. But no doubt the truth was that, with his natural wisdom and discernment of the fitness of things, he recognized the wide difference between him and Mary Wilson, in education and culture, which was not so marked when they were children together. At all events he did not appear to possess any lasting sentimental thoughts for her who was the companion of his childhood, and in a couple of years after this incident married another woman, who for fifty years was his faithful helpmeet.

CHAPTER IX.

AT the age of twenty-three or four (his exact age we are unable to ascertain) Nat followed the example of his brother Elisha and "committed matrimony." The young woman he selected for his partner in life was Jemima Streeter, daughter of one Amos Streeter. Jeptha R. Simms, in a short sketch of the life of our hero in his book, "Trappers of New York," copyrighted in 1850, makes the statement that Miss Jemima was a New Hampshire lass; but we are authoritatively informed by descendants of Foster, that she was a New York girl, and that she came from St. Lawrence county, her father being a justice of that county. The details of Nat's courtship and marriage are very meager, so meager in fact, that I have none at all. But as this event in its generalities is the same in the life of any man, be he prince or pauper, we can well afford to pass over this feature of his life and meet him again as he is settled on his own farm at Salisbury, Herkimer county, New York.

In person he was, as I have mentioned, about

six feet tall, erect and strongly built, possessing a muscular frame that seemed well adapted for enduring the fatigues of the chase. His features were commanding, though not handsome. His eyes were blue and had a merry twinkle. Long before his face would relax into a smile, his expressive eyes would tell of the approaching manifestation of pleasure. This pleasant peculiarity he retained all through his life.

The country around his new home at Salisbury was mostly a wilderness and alive with game. Indeed, one of the chief reasons, we may believe, for his leaving the associations of his relation, and with his young wife seeking a new home farther in the wilderness, was that he might follow with greater success his favorite avocation, hunting and trapping.

From the time he settled at Salisbury, until the tragedy at the Old Forge in his old age, he followed the fortunes of a hunter with marked success. In justice to him I must state that all through his long career he never neglected his farm at Salisbury. In a few years after his settlement there he possessed a farm of one hundred and fifty acres, which received his careful attention. He grew annually good-sized crops of grain. Wheat, buckwheat, rye and oats being among the cereals he raised. He would always

sell his surplus grain at a reasonable figure, paying no attention to the market prices for these
commodities, though always posted on the mar-
ketable value of furs and pelts. Very often, I
am told, when the prices of grain were high, and
the winters severe, he would load a sleigh with
bags of grain, and going about the surrounding
country, give a couple of bags to every poor
family whose home he passed, and in the spring
any one could get seeding from him for nothing,
if he had it to spare.

For a long time he conducted an "ashery" for
the making of potash in connection with his
farming, employing men to collect the ashes and
do the work for him. Wood being the only fuel
of the time, wood ashes were plentiful and easily
obtained. From them was made the potash referred to. The ashes were put in leaches, simply
old barrels or boxes with troughs underneath;
water was then filtered through them which,
after soaking through the ashes, ran from the
troughs a stong lye. The lye thus obtained was
then boiled down and poured into pot shaped
moulds, from whence the name pot-ash was obtained. These crystals were then shipped to
Albany, where the material was manufactured
into pearl ash and soda ash. He also had a large
fish pond on his farm where he kept trout that

he might always be able to give his friends a treat when they visited him by serving fresh trout at some meal.

I mention these various facts connected with his farm to show that he was an industrious, benevolent citizen, and in no sense a shiftless, indolent hunter and trapper. His excursions into the woods every autumn and winter for hunting and trapping were matters of business fully as much as pleasure for him. For thirty years he thus lived at Salisbury, leading the life of a hunter, trapper and farmer. He raised a large family of children, for whom he provided carefully and conscientiously.

When he settled at Salisbury he could neither read nor write. But some time after his settlement there, one of the storekeepers of the village taught him to write his name, and from this accomplishment he branched out into arithmetic and reading, mastering the rudiments of both, with the help of the storekeeper and his wife.

In a year or two after he settled at Salisbury, his father and brother Elisha moved from the east and settled with their families in the same town, so that Nat took up his hunting again with Elisha, though it does not appear that they companioned in this pursuit as much as before; but his youngest brothers, Elihu and Shubael, very frequently accompanied him in his hunting and trapping excursions deep into the forests.

At the time Nat emigrated to Herkimer county, game was so abundant that with his fondness for the sport, together with the inducements offered for hunting by the bounties paid for wolves, black bears and panthers, his pursuit of game was a source of great profit. He began his pioneer residence in the winter and by spring he had taken enough fur, mostly beaver, I am told, to purchase a cow and many articles necessary to housekeeping and farming. He afterwards obtained yearly large quantities of valuable fur, such as beaver, otter, martin, fisher and muskrat. It was nothing for him to have several hundred traps set in a single season during the years when he was in his prime and the game abundant. He of course, employed men to assist him in such stupendous work, paying them good wages, and having a fair margin left for his own profit. Deers, bears, wolves and panthers were so numerous about Salisbury for years after he made his home on the borders of the woods, that he slaughtered them in great numbers. It is believed to be justly said that he killed more of these animals collectively than any other white man in the State, having slain

no less than seventy-five deer in one season and
ninety-six bears in three seasons. Wolves he
killed and trapped in large numbers. One season, when the bounty on them was high, he had
two lines of wolf traps extending from Salisbury into the very heart of the Adirondacks;
some say it extended clear through the wilderness to the St. Lawrence river. This is not improbable, considering his general extensive
operations, and the fact that some of the adventures he had, which we will note, occurred
in the county of St. Lawrence.

The avails of his hunting and trapping
amounted one season, when a liberal bounty was
paid on wolves, bears and panthers, and he had
taken an unusual number of furs of other animals, to twelve hundred dollars, which he had in
gold in the spring after he had closed up all of
his sales and accounts. This was a vast sum
for those days.

The bounties paid for the destruction of wild
animals often made the town taxes something
of a burden. One year a quite wealthy farmer
took a stand at the town meeting against paying
so large a bounty as was then paid, and succeeded in securing a large reduction in the
prices paid by the officers for bears' tails, wolves'
heads and panthers' ears. At this all the hunt-

ers of the township turned their attention to other game and purposely let the wolves and panthers alone. In a year's time they had greatly increased, the wolves particularly coming from the interior of the wilderness in great numbers attracted to the settlements by the toothsome, and now more easily obtained sheep. Foster had told his wealthy neighbor that he would be sorry for the manner in which he had worked and voted at the town meeting. And after the animals had had time to increase, he was not surprised one day to be told a most pitiful story by the same farmer, of the injuries and loss he had sustained the night before by wolves, which had gotten into his sheep fold and destroyed more property than his tax had amounted to when the bounty for wolf scalps was the highest. But the farmer found he was "barking up the wrong tree" when he told his tale to Foster, for after listening to him a moment he interrupted him by saying, "Well, I don't know as I can pity you. If you are not willing to pay me for protecting your sheep, you must buy traps and take care of them yourself." The penurious farmer saw the point; and it is needless to say was ready to vote a more liberal bounty than ever at the next town meeting.

The winter that the bounty was off the wild

animals of a destructive nature, Foster turned
his attention entirely to the killing of deer and
moose, disposing of many of their carcasses in
the eastern market. There may be seen now in
Albany, New York and Philadelphia museums,
mounted specimens of noble deer and moose
killed by this famous hunter. He at one time
had a captive moose on his farm at Salisbury,
keeping it stalled in his barn.

Foster for a time carried a rifle called a
"double shooter," made after a pattern designed
by a gunsmith of the village, named Willis
Avery, whose descendants still live in the village.
The guns were made with single barrels, but
with two locks, one above the other, and far
enough apart to admit of two charges, the upper
charge of powder resting against the lower bullet. The locks were made for percussion pills,
and when the pick was down which crushed the
pill at the upper lock, there was no danger to be
apprehended in firing the other charge. In prac-
tical use, howver, it was found that the vents
would become plugged with a few firings, and
they would have to be patiently picked open with
a pin. So that the guns, which were really very
ingenious, and would have answered admirably
if percussion caps had been known, never came
into general use. The rifle which Foster used

most of his life would carry two balls as well as one. It was made expressly for him by Mr. Avery, and was light at the muzzle and heavy at the breech. This, Foster explained, was for the purpose of shooting game on the move. When he wished to make game doubly sure he would load with two bullets. It was in this manner he loaded it when he shot the Indian at the Old Forge.

He was remarkably expert at loading and firing his rifle. Particularly so if it was necessary to make several shots in hot haste and at short range. He was frequently known upon a wager to commence with his rifle unloaded and fire it off six times in one minute. This seems almost incredible, but nevertheless it is true. And we better understand it when we are told how he carried his bullets and loaded and fired on such occasions. He would place three well pared balls between the fingers of each hand; then from a powder horn provided with a charger, he would pour in the powder, drop in a ball which would just roll down the barrel without a patch, strike the butt of the gun with his hand, which primed it, and the next instant the bullet was speeding to its mark. Of course, this could be done only in firing at short range. To make long shots, it was necessary to patch

the balls and drive them home with a ramrod.
A flint-lock rifle, of course, was used. His large
bony hand aided him in retaining bullets between his fingers, and as he began early to thus
carry them, they formed for themselves cavities,
the tissue of his fingers forming itself into almost
the exact shape of a bullet mould, which nearly
concealed the lead between his fingers. He was
able to manipulate his gun, handle his knife or
an ax without removing them. An ordinary
observer, even in shaking hands with him, would
not have noticed the strange jewelry he wore.

"A regiment of such riflemen as Foster firing
at close range," says Simms in his book, "would
soon decide the fate of a battle." Which was
quite true for those days.

In the second American war with Great Britain, the following incident is related of Foster
by his youngest brother, Shubael: "A company
of riflemen from South Carolina, commanded by
Captain Forsyth, passed through the town of
Salisbury, near Diamond Hill, two miles north
of Salisbury Corners. The troops were on their
way from the Mohawk Valley to the military
lines between New York and Canada. They encamped at Manheim over one day for the purpose of washing their clothes. The celebrity of
Foster as a rapid shooter and accurate marks-

12

man came to the ears of Captain Forsyth, and he sent for Foster and questioned him in regard to his ability to fulfill all the extraordinary stories told by his friends about him. Foster did not have much to say, merely telling the captain that he would wager that he could "put more balls into the bigness of a man in the space of one minute than any one in his command." Now, Captain Forsyth had in his company a most expert and rapid rifleman named Robinson, and so he immediately took Foster at his word and arranged to have him pitted against his crack marksman. The terms of the wager were agreed upon and the manner of the test settled. They were to shoot six times at targets ten rods away, each beginning with unloaded rifle at the same time. They took their places, with the company drawn up in line to witness, as they supposed the defeat of the lank and uncouth trapper. Foster had his six well pared rifle balls between his fingers, which were unobserved.

"The signal was given and they began. Foster made things hum for a minute, while he poured the powder from his horn into the gun, mysteriously spread his fingers over the muzzle of his rifle, knocked the butt gently on the palm of his hand, and blazed away at his target, always putting a ball there, though where it

came from none could imagine. He put the
sixth ball in his target, having made a little circle of six holes in the piece of bark, while Robinson was still fumbling in his bullet pouch for his
fourth bullet. A murmur of applause ran
through the ranks, and Foster was at once a lion
in the camp. Captain Forsyth was greatly surprised at finding so skillful and rapid a marksman on the frontier of New York, and anxious
to secure his service, he offered him thirty dollars a month to join his company with the com-
plimentary assurance that he might eat at his table.
But as the war was regarded as nearly over, and
Foster in common with many men of the interior, did not approve of the war anyway, he
declined the offer."

Foster was sometimes accompanied by another hunter in his excursions into the woods.
Occasionally he would devote a season to the
business in partnership with another, at the end
dividing the spoils or the proceeds of their sale.
Stoner, who was a warm friend of Foster's from
the time of his gallant conduct at St. Johnsville
on the Fourth of July, sometimes visited him at
Salisbury and accompanied him on his hunts.
But more often than not he threaded the track-
less forests alone.

His accoutrements for a long journey, like

going to the Fulton Chain or the most northern
lakes, were quite numerous. Slung from his
left shoulder and hanging at his right side would
be a large powder horn and bullet pouch of suf-
ficient dimensions to warrant a lengthy hunt. A
belt encircled his waist, through which was thrust
a sheathed knife with keen edge, and an ax or
hatchet. When on jaunts for trapping, a bundle
of small steel traps would also be suspended from
his right shoulder. To his back was strapped
his pack basket, containing his blanket, perhaps
some more traps, a tin teapot, and sheet-iron
frying pan, a supply of tea, salt, Indian meal,
and in the early part of the trip some bread.

When tramping through the forests he could
make his camp in thirty minutes, with the snow
even a foot deep. He would set up two
crotched sticks, stretch a pole across them, and
others from this to the ground, then covering the
whole with hemlock boughs, and closing the
sides with the same and strewing a liberal supply of twigs on the ground or snow, as the case
might be, a good shelter was provided for his
night's repose. According to the expression of
an old guide, whom I interviewed, and
who remembers Foster, the roof of such a hut
properly thatched with hemlock boughs to the
depth of six or eight inches, "would shed all the
water that ever fell in Noah's flood."

"A good shelter * * * for his night's repose."

It might not be as water-tight as that, but I have no doubt that it would shed all the water that fell in the hardest kind of a thunder shower. Building a huge fire before the open front of the shanty, Foster would spread his blanket on the fragrant boughs, and rolling himself therein, would sleep soundly until morning, or until awakened by the howl or bark of wild animals.

He never carried a compass with him in the woods, yet he was never lost, being always able to readily locate the directions by observing the tops of some near-by hemlock tree. He maintained that the small tapering top of these trees always grew with a slight bending towards the east, caused by the western winds; so he had only to look to the top of one of these trees of the forest and then go confidently on his way. If one of these trees was not in view, as sometimes might happen, then he studied the bark of any tree; even the drifting of the snow in winter afforded him means of guidance.

As he grew older and his reputation as a hunter and trapper increased, his kind and genial manner, which he coupled with all of his exploits, won for him the title of "Uncle Nat." And by this name he was called by people far and near, by those who knew him personally and by those who knew him by reputation only. His fame for shooting was increased in his younger days by his once delivering two girls from the attack of a panther. They were out in the woods in the vicinity of Salisbury, gathering flowers. Accompanying them was a large Newfoundland dog, named Towser. As they were strolling along, with Towser ahead, they saw what they supposed was another dog of a different kind, come out of the brush and commence to play and gambol with Towser. He, however, was not so inclined to play as was the strange dog, but instead commenced to growl and show his teeth and finally ended the sport by seizing the stranger by the throat and shaking the life out of him.

The girls watched the struggle with interest, and when Towser threw the vanquished animal from him they clapped their hands in applause. But their pleasure was soon turned to fear, for Towser had scarcely turned to trot back to the girls to be petted by them for his success, when another of the same kind of brutes, only much larger, sprang from the brush and attacked the dog. It was an uneven struggle, and though poor Towser made a gallant fight, he soon began to weaken. The oldest girl now divined the true nature of the animal their dog was struggling with. It was a fierce and ugly panther, and it was her young one Towser had slain. This she did not dare to tell her companion for fear she would scream and, perhaps, faint, leaving them both entirely at the mercy of the wild beast.

In silence they watched the battle between their faithful canine friend and the huge yellow cat. Towser fought fearlessly and gave the panther a hard tussle before he was vanquished. At last the panther gained the mastery, and securing a hold on the dog's throat, dealt with him as its own kitten had been dealt with but a moment before. Then crouching over the body of the poor dog, it fastened its devilish eyes on the now terrified girls. By this time the youngest girl had also guessed the true nature of the animal that was struggling with their dog. And as she saw the struggle between them cease, and Towser dead, with the panther preparing to spring on them, she uttered a scream and fell fainting into the arms of her companion.

This brave girl who had witnessed the struggle with so much fortitude, now gave herself and her fainting friend up as lost. Supporting her prostrate companion, she bowed her head and waited the spring of the awful beast. But the scream the fainting girl had uttered was their salvation. Foster was in the vicinity, gun in hand, and hearing the agonized cry, hastened towards the spot from whence it came. He came in sight of the startling tableau of the huddling girls and crouching panther just as the latter was about to spring. Quick as a flash he raised his rifle, and observing that the head of the oldest girl covered the sight of the rifle, he uttered a warning "hist" and gently told her to lower her head. The girl heard and heeded. She suffered her head to sink upon her breast, and the next instant Foster's rifle spoke their deliverance. He had put the ball squarely between the panther's eyes and it dropped dead upon the body of the dog it had slain. .

No doubt my readers will recognize this story. Where have you seen it? In Cooper's Leatherstocking Tales. This incident in the life of Foster, it appears, the famous novelist has woven into the fabric of his thrilling adventures of Leatherstocking. But I believe this is the only incident in Foster's life that can be discovered in Cooper's works. In a foot note in the book "The Deerslayer," this incident is credited to Otsego county. But Foster's family say that it occurred in Herkimer county, and near Salisbury. Simms in his book calls Foster "the modern Leatherstocking." He seemed ignorant of the fact that in a sense he was the Leatherstocking of Cooper. And indeed, I have every reason to believe that Foster was the identical character used by Cooper in his "Leatherstocking Tales." One of his descendants made this assertion to me, which I was at first inclined to discredit. But from the similarity of the two characters, I unintentionally obtained in gathering the facts of Foster's life, I became convinced that Nat Foster is Cooper's "Natty Bumfo." I am not alone in this opinion. The late Judge Hurlbut, who defended Foster at his trial for killing the Indian at the Old Forge, and who had known Foster for years, was of this opinion. His son, Gansevort de W. Hurlbut of Albany, N. Y., is also of the same opinion, based upon statements of his father, and his own comparison of the two characters. In a letter to me bearing on this subject, Mr. Hurlbut says: "James Fennimore Cooper having known Foster in his lifetime (at an early age) it seems not improbable that he took Foster as the original of his famous scout and trapper, commonly called 'Leatherstocking,' or in other words, that 'Nat Foster' and 'Natty Bumfo' were identical. Observe the similarity in description, of manners, habits and person. Dread of the law, and consequent outward conformity; their laughing in an exactly similar manner, without noise; mouth the same; the style

of rifle carried by both; both leaving the state;
*   *   *   *   and through it all, you find points
of similarity, hardly the work of chance. After
the comparison of the Leatherstocking in the
'Pioneers,' and the 'Deerslayer' with the character of Foster as described by Simms, and there
is additional ground for the assertion that they
are the same persons; or rather, that Cooper's
hero was none other than Nat Foster." This
is the statement of a man who knows whereof
he speaks. If my work amounts to nothing
more, I will be satisfied, if it develops into a bio-
graphy of the man who afforded the inspiration
to Cooper to write those thrilling and fascinating
"Leatherstocking Tales," which have delighted
and entertained so many of us from our youth,
even until now.

CHAPTER X.

I WILL now devote a couple of chapters to the relating of stories and anecdotes of Foster's life while hunting in the Adirondacks, as they have been preserved in the memory of his own family.

Countless stories of his life and adventures may be had at any time without the asking from the mouths of old guides and residents of the region. Many of them are marvelous; some of them are stupid and very thin on their face. It was always my practice to take them with "a grain of salt and an ounce of consideration." When I set out to write a history of Foster's life, it was my determination, which I have adhered to, to produce only such stories as were authenticated by a member of some branch of his family; but I must confess that even some of these authenticated and thus reliable stories staggered me by their startling, and at first sight, unreasonable statement. So the reader must not be incredulous at the sometimes sudden surprises and unexpected results of Foster's experiences, as perhaps you may already have been. For it was over half a century ago that Foster hunted and trapped, when the Adirondacks were fairly teeming with all kinds of game common to that region in its original and natural state. The wilderness was really and truly a "forest primeval." Foster was among the first of the white men who invested it for the pecuniary gain its wealth of animal life afforded. The dusky Indian, it is true, had hunted and trapped there for centuries, but apparently had made no impression on the multitudinous and varied kinds of animals that abounded. They were many, and nearly all were valuable in one way or another to a hunter like Foster, who followed the fortunes of the chase for nearly half of every year, as an honest and agreeable means of contributing to his support.

There were the small animals like the martin and fisher, together with the fox, that were caught with traps and dead-falls anywhere in the woods. Then there were the otter, beaver and muskrat, caught with steel traps along streams and around lakes and ponds. These animals were valuable because of their fur. The larger animals were desired either because of the bounty paid by the towns and the State for their destruction, or because of the value of their car-

"Another creature * * * that often made things lively for our hero."

casses for food. It was with the larger game, like the deer, moose, bear, panther and wolf, which were as plentiful as the smaller game, that Foster had his most exciting and interesting experiences. And it was about such adventures as I have stated, that I was the most surprised and doubtful. Yet, upon second thought, we can see it was nothing strange when these animals cut up the most wonderful freaks with him when he trespassed into their lairs in pursuit of them.

In this connection I say nothing about another creature that would not justly come under the head of the quadruped, but which nevertheless often made things lively for our hero as he was threading the forests after game with four legs. I leave the reader to discover its species. It often figures in his most exciting exploits in the Adirondacks, as it already has in one or two of his adventures as a lad and as a young man.

One time as he was hunting in Herkimer county, following up the banks of Spruce creek, he came upon two noble bucks browsing upon the tender shoots of bushes that overhung the banks of the creek. He readily shot one of them, but the other bounded off into the brush. Determined to secure it, he dragged the carcass of the one he had, out of the water onto the bank and then followed the trail of the other deer in hopes of starting it again; after going a mile without success, he abandoned the attempt, and returned to secure the one he had shot. Imagine his surprise upon gaining the bank of the creek again to find the deer gone. It took him but a moment, however, to ascertain its whereabouts. It had been dragged into the bushes and carefully covered with dead leaves. His practiced eye told him at once that it was the work of some wild animal, probably a panther. He resolved at once to fool the beast, and secure its own head in the bargain. Quickly removing the carcass of the deer, he replaced it with pieces of an old rotten log, then having made everything about the heap as nearly as possible as it was before, he concealed himself in a clump of bushes near by and waited to see what the results would be.

In a short time his patience was rewarded by beholding an old she panther with two young ones approaching; coming to within a few rods of the pile of leaves, she halted the young ones and advancing cat-like, to within twenty feet of the pile, gave a spring, landing squarely on the pile of leaves and commenced to scatter them in all directions. In a moment she had uncovered, not the toothsome carcass of a sleek deer, but an old rotten and decayed log.

"She was the most disappointed and astonished animal I ever saw," said Foster in relating the adventure. "She stood still and looked first about her, and then at the log. She would sniff the air and then the billet of wood she stood on, and the poor kittens a few rods away, were all the time looking on, in wonderment, I suppose, at their mother's strange actions. Suddenly she seemed to discover me, for she screamed as they always do, and crouched down to spring in my direction. I thought now it was about time to begin action, and so gave her a charge between the eyes; she never even moved from the log, but dropped dead where she crouched. I then easily got the kittens and think I did a pretty good afternoon's work, getting a deer and the three panther heads, which brought me a good bounty."

Foster's stories of unexpected good luck, and of "lucky shots," whereby he would secure a large and varied amount of game, are remarkable. One of them relates to the bagging inside of a couple of hours, of two wolves, five panthers and one deer. This wonderful achievement was accomplished when he was tramping through the woods near Panther Lake.

As he was making his solitary way through the forests, his course was arrested by a deer coming through the brush pursued by a wolf, or perhaps by a whole pack. He allowed the deer to cross the trail without firing, but waited with cocked rifle for the appearance of its pursurers. He was obliged to wait but a few moments when a couple of huge wolves, their tongues hanging out, their breasts and shoulders flecked with foam, came crashing into view. The foremost brute no sooner leaped into sight than a bullet from the Nimrod's rifle stopped its course forever, and it was but an instant more ere the other was similarly dealt with.

Here was luck. The scalps of the two wolves were worth sixty dollars. With a "humph" of satisfaction, Foster carefully reloaded his rifle with a patched ball and setting it within easy reach, commenced to skin the wolves. As he was busily engaged in this occupation his quick ear detected the approach of wild animals, and looking up, he saw not five rods from him a female panther and two half-grown ones. They had been attracted to the spot by the smell of fresh meat. It was but the work of an instant to snatch his rifle and send a ball through the old one's head: then he quickly dispatched the two young ones.

He now had more game to skin, and so he set to work to finish the wolves. Being an experienced hunter he did not relax his vigilance in

the least, for he knew that when the mother panther was around there was likely to be in the
vicinity her mate with a part of the family, so
setting his rifle within his reach he busied himself with the work of skinning the animals, until,
as he expected, he heard another cracking in the
bushes, and looking up, he beheld, what he afterwards declared to be the biggest panther he ever
saw in his life. It was followed closely by another half-grown one, like the two he had already
shot. They were both making towards him on a
trot, with their necks stretched out and heads
erect, presenting excellent shots. In fact, both
opportunities for shooting being so good, he
was in doubt as he picked up his rifle again
which to shoot first; but as he raised his gun the
sight covered the young one, and he let drive at
it, dropping it in its very tracks. The old one
gave an awful scream and sprang onto the inclined trunk of a half prostrate tree that was but
a few feet away. As it ran up the trunk of the
tree it presented a fine shot, and Foster, who
with his usual rapidity of loading, had quickly
dropped into his gun a charge of powder and a
ball from between his fingers, now gave him a
charge; to his astonishment the beast kept on
his course up the tree. At first he thought he
had missed him, yet wondered how that could

13

be, as his rifle never made a miss. Before he had time to fire again, the panther had run to the end of the tree and dropped off onto the ground, where it lay motionless, in fact dead. An examination showed the hunter that he had shot it, as he had intended, through the head, and only muscular action could have carried it to the end of the tree.

Foster now surveyed the field of battle and counted up the spoils. He had two dead wolves, and five panther carcasses, as a result of the deer chase. He now bethought himself of the deer, and recollecting that he needed fresh and edible meat at his camp, he resolved to possess himself of the deer. He knew if it had been run far by the wolves, before he rid it of those troublesome enemies, it would be resting somewhere on the shore of the lake. Accordingly he set out on the trail the fleeing deer had made, and as he had expected, the deer was lying in the bushes on the lake shore. It started up on his approach, to flee away. Putting away the thought of pity, which prompted him to spare the timid creature when it crossed his trail, he brought it down with a charge from his rifle.

He dressed the deer, and then returned to the scene of action and finished taking the hides from the panthers and wolves. By the time he had gotten all of the spoils to his camp that night he was both hungry and tired. He started a fire and soon had some choice cuts from the deer roasting on a spit, and as he ate the savory meat seasoned with a pinch of salt, he had no regrets for the fate of the poor deer that had brought him such good luck that day.

Foster himself said that in all of his trapping and hunting experiences he was frightened but once, and that was one time when he came across two young bear cubs in the woods. They were a lively pair, and when the hunter discovered them, were crawling about on some logs, eating red raspberries from bushes that overhung the logs. Foster decided not to molest them for the time being, but wait for their parent to put in her appearance. So he seated himself on a convenient log under the shade of a friendly tree, for the day was sultry, and before he knew it, dropped off into a doze. While thus drowsing the old bear he was to watch for appeared on the scene, and espying the nodding hunter she ambled towards him, and coming up to the end of the log on which Foster was seated, she placed her immense forepaws on it and uttered a fearful growl, at the same time giving the log a shake which nearly precipitated the hunter to the ground. It is said that dreams are instantaneous impressions of the mind. Whether it was a dream or not, Foster thought for a moment that the bear was on his back, and in his consternation and fear he leaped, he said, at least a dozen feet before he discovered that the bear was not on his back but many feet away from him. Becoming thoroughly awakened, he ceased his inglorious flight and, turning, sent a ball from his trusty rifle through her heart.

It is believed that this was the only time he was ever caught really "napping" by either man or beast. According to his own statement it is. And certain it is that the wily Indian who ordinarily was so shrewd, was often outwitted by this keen and sharp pale-face, and was never caught napping by them.

It is related of him that he was once attacked in the forests by an Indian intent on killing him. They both took refuge behind trees, and from their respective positions kept up a fusilade all the afternoon without either gaining the advantage. As it became dusk, the shrewd old hunter removed his coon skin cap and his coat, and arranging his rifle with them so that it looked like a figure of a man, he cautiously pushed the effigy out from behind the beech tree which sheltered him. The cap and coat had not been in the view of the savage a quarter of a minute before he shot at it, supposing in the dusk of the evening that he had put a ball into the body of his antagonist. To complete the deception, Foster gave a death-like groan and caused the cap and coat to sway back and forth a moment and then to fall slowly to the ground. The Indian, now supposing that he had surely brought down his man, gave a whoop of triumph, rushed forward from his tree, knife in hand, to scalp the fallen foe. This was what Foster wanted. The poor Indian had not proceeded a rod from his tree before the crack of the hunter's rifle undeceived him, if undeceived he could be, for a bullet had pierced his brain.

Another time as Foster was traveling through the wilderness in the vicinity of Indian river, his dog Watch, manifested some uneasiness. Like his mother Rose, who was long since dead, Watch could scent either four-legged or two-legged game at a good distance. On this occasion he scented game, but of which kind his master was not sure. From the dog's actions, and from the fact that he was laden with furs, he suspected it was an Indian intent on killing him and taking his pack.

Coming to a little hill he made a detour around it and came up again on his own trail and found it was as he suspected. From tracks in the light snow he saw that he was being followed by an Indian, for in addition to his own tracks there were those of another with the tell-tale "turn in" impression made by an Indian foot. He waited for nothing more. Calling his old coon-skin cap into use again, he placed it on an old log that crossed his trail, so that the top was just visible to one approaching, thus presenting the appearance that the owner and wearer was concealed behind the log. Then with his dog he crouched behind a hemlock and waited for the Indian's approach opposite.

In a little while he saw the Indian making his way along, studying the trail. He had followed Foster's trail around the hill and now came upon the old trail again. He seemed a little puzzled as he now came to the three tracks in the snow, and stopped and looked cautiously around. His eyes finally rested upon the fur cap appearing just above the top of the log; supposing it to be on the head of the owner he raised his rifle, took deliberate aim and fired. Simultaneously with the discharge of his own rifle, however, another one sent forth its small thunder, and the merciless Indian fell back as if kicked dead by his own gun.

The Sacandaga river was the scene of several of Foster's encounters with the Indians. As we have seen, when he was only twenty-one he had such a serious brush with them on this river that he "frightened" them away. But his victory on that occasion did not prevent many of their fellows from bothering him afterwards.

One time he was operating along the west branch of the river, having traps set in the woods for mink and fisher, and along the banks of the stream for otter and muskrat. He also had a number of traps set around the Trout lakes, where he was having wonderfully good success in taking fisher and otter, together with a beaver or two every night from the colonies that were at the outlets of the lakes. Finally his success here ceased, and every morning his traps would be empty, but with every evidence of having done service during the night. So he determined to watch for the intruders and settle with the thieves.

There was a foot bridge across the river about thirty rods below where the outlet of the lakes emptied into the river. It was nothing but the trunk of an old tree, but it had fallen in such a convenient position across the river as to be appropriated as a foot bridge. Foster always crossed upon this in going to attend to his traps at the lakes, and he presumed those who were stealing from his traps there, would also. So making his way to the river one morning, before the break of day, he concealed himself behind the upturned roots of the prostrate "monarch of the forest," which were on the side of the river towards the lakes. From this position he could wait and watch for the ones who would be coming to inspect his traps along the outlet stream at the lakes.

Before it was fairly light he saw two figures coming stealing along towards the log across the river. Said Foster, in relating the adventure, "I watched 'em as they came towards the bridge and felt sure they were the ones who had been stealing from my traps. They were Injuns anyhow, I was sure of that. They came onto the bridge over the flowing stream and I raised my rifle and covered 'em with the sight, and thought —how easy it would be to shoot both on 'em at once. But as I was thinking thus they both had got to the middle of the log, where they appeared to get dizzy, for they both fell into the stream below. And," he concluded with a significant shake of his head, "they didn't bother my traps after that."

When trapping in this section of the country after the Upper Mill was built, which was situated about two miles from the place where the above tragedy occurred, Foster would make his headquarters with the operators of the sawmill, as it was far better than camping in the woods. The mill pond also contained otters and muskrats to be trapped and snared.

Foster's reputation as an Indian slayer was well understood by both white men and red men who lived in the woods. The former took it as a matter of course, and from the old trapper's reluctance to talk about these events of his life they seldom mentioned them when in his presence. The Indians, on the contrary, and as we might expect, resented this thinning out of their race by "Ole Nat Foster," as they called him. Many were the Indians who set out on his track to shoot him only to be shot themselves.

One morning as Foster was standing by the mill in question, engaged in conversation with a group of mill hands, a ferocious looking Indian came into the clearing and approached the men. He was clad in the regulation hunting dress of an Indian, which was scarcely a dress at all, for it consisted of only a pair of short buckskin breeches, which did not cover the loins, a pair of leggings and moccasins. A belt encircled his waist, supporting the breeches, and carrying a knife and hatchet. At his side hung a powder horn and bullet pouch. A very dirty blanket was drawn about his bare shoulders. The only

attractive thing about the dusky warrior was a
bright new rifle he carried.

Coming to the group of men he addressed
them in a most haughty manner, as if desirous
of impressing them with the fact that he was
especially bedecked and armed for the warpath.
The first thing he said was to inquire if "Ole
Nat Foster" was about. The men were a little
amused but made no answer, looking to Foster
to reply.

Foster gave a significant wink to his companions and told the dusky stranger that he was
not, but had already gone to look after his traps.

"Where be his traps," asked the Indian, a
gleam of anticipation coming into his eye.

"Wal," said Foster, "his line o' traps begin
over thar, by the end of the pond. But say,"
he added as the Indian turned to go, "that's a
fine gun you've got thar, let's have a look at it."

It was indeed a fine-looking firearm and an
Indian owner would naturally be anxious to
show it. But he shook his head, and turning
again to go, said, "No, me go and shoot ole Foster first, then I come back and show you gun."

"But can you shoot," asked Foster, "old Foster is a dead shot, and you want to look out."

"Oh, me good shot, me not afraid," answered
the Indian, confidently.

"Oh, pshaw," said Foster, "I'll bet I can beat you, let's have a try."

"You good shot?" asked the Indian, as he eyed the old trapper curiously.

"Well, just try and see who is the best," answered Foster.

At this the Indian appeared inclined to try; but recollecting himself, he shook his head and repeated that he must first go and shoot old Foster, when he would return and try his hand with the stranger. At last, however, Foster and his companions prevailed upon the Indian to shoot with Foster and exhibit his superior skill and his rifle, of both of which he seemed very vain.

A proper distance was at once paced off and a target set up, and the Indian took his place for the first shot, never suspecting that his rival was the very man he was so desirous of shooting. He made his shot showing fair skill as a marksman.

"Now," said Foster, as he took the rifle from the Indian, "you go and plug up the hole you made, so there won't be no mistake by my possibly shooting in the same place."

Without the least suspicion the Indian started for the target. It was but the work of an instant for Foster to load the rifle and the next instant, before he ever reached it, the Indian was bored between the shoulders with a ball from his own rifle. When the Hamilton county officials investigated the matter, the affair was reported as "accidental." Foster being unused to the gun had handled it in such a way that it was discharged, and of course the Indian received the charge. This seemed to satisfy the authorities, and Foster was never brought before a court for the deed.

An interesting story is told in Simms' book of the dog Watch, mentioned in this chapter. The animal figured in many of Foster's exploits during the first few years of his master's residence in Salisbury. The dog was dammed by the bitch Rose, which was with him on his trip to Piesco Lake the time he captured little Mary French from the Indians, and "sent her captors back to Canada," as he expressed it.

Watch was as fond of hunting as was his master, and often went on a hunt for himself. "One day the bay of this sagacious animal," says Simms, "called the owner to a retired spot in the forest, where he discovered Watch holding a moose by the nose, keeping his own body between the forelegs of his adversary to avoid the heavy blows aimed at him with the antlers of the enraged animal, which formidable weapons weighed nearly thirty pounds.

"Upon coming to the spot Foster sent a bullet into the head of the moose, which in its death struggle dashed the dog off with terrific force, throwing the brave dog against the trunk of a tree. The print of the dog's teeth remained upon the nose of the moose, but he himself appeared to be dead. Foster took off his coat and spreading it on the ground, laid his canine friend upon it. About this time a partner in the hunt arrived upon the scene and they prepared to dress the moose.

"With a heavy heart Foster began to whet his knife, when his comrade noticed a twitching of the muscles about the dog's neck, and he tried to cheer Foster by telling him the dog would recover. The old hunter shook his head doubtingly and set about the task of getting the moose ready to hang up and skin. As his master was engaged in this occupation, Watch raised his head slowly from the ground; at this Foster at once left off his work and began to caress him. Watch returned his attention gratefully, until his eye rested upon the body of his fallen foe, when springing to his feet he seized the lifeless moose by the throat from which he could only be removed with considerable difficulty. This restoration of his favorite dog to life and vigor caused Foster more real joy than the killing of a dozen moose could possibly have done."

CHAPTER XI.

MANY of Foster's exploits, like a few recorded in the preceding chapter, occurred in the vicinity of his own home, while others occurred farther away, in the very heart of the Adirondacks. As deer and moose grew scarce near his home, he and his brothers would penetrate into other districts in the fall in quest of this game for their winter's supply of meat.

The following incident occurred while he and his brother Shubael were on a deer hunt in St. Lawrence county, and will serve to show the numberless perils to which he exposed himself in those days. The two hunters were making their way stealthily along through the dense forests "still hunting," when they came suddenly upon two noble bucks engaged in combat, probably trying titles to the territory.

To end this dispute and give his brother a chance to shoot some noble game, Foster told Shubael to "shoot the nigh deer." The lad obeyed; he fired and the nigh deer dropped.

"That's good; now shoot the other one," exclaimed his brother as he whipped out his knife and rushed forward to stick the fallen deer.

The other buck had bounded off as Shubael fired, but now stopped to witness, with the terrified Shubael, who forgot all about shooting again, a more novel engagement than the recent one. The fallen buck was not killed, but only stunned by the ball from Shubael's rifle striking it in the neck, near the spinal cord. As Foster ran up to cut its throat, the animal sprang to its feet and began to strike furiously at the hardy hunter with its powerful antlers. Quick as a flash, Foster placed the knife between his teeth and grasped the weapons of his foe. Then began a struggle for the mastery, more furious than the two bucks' engagement; one which for a time paralyzed Shubael, charmed the uninjured buck, who remained a few rods away gazing upon the scene, and caused the squirrels and chipmunks to scurry to their holes in alarm at the unusual confusion. Foster maintained his grip upon the antlers of the deer while the animal thrashed him about among the trees and bushes in an alarming manner. The struggle was long and fierce, Foster not daring to let go his hold, nor even *willing* to give up until he had gained the mastery. Finally, as good luck would have it, he got the head of the deer wedged between two trees, against one of which a horn was broken, and the worried animal thrown down, when he quickly cut its throat with the knife he had kept firmly clutched between his teeth.

As the confusion ceased and quiet reigned again, the other buck made known the fact that he had been a silent spectator by leaping through the underbrush.

At this Foster, who had risen and was wiping the blood and dirt from his face, exclaimed to his brother, disgustedly, "I thought you'd shoot the other one! Geme the gun," and, snatching it from his brother's hand, he raised it, sighted a patch of the fleeing deer among the leaves of the forest, fired and brought it down.

The tussle between Foster and the wounded deer, I am told, lasted over ten minutes. The ground was trampled and the grass and bushes beaten down for rods around, and his tattered garments must have reminded him of certain engagements of his youth.

One time he had an amusing experience with a trapped bear and a very confident neighbor near his own home at Salisbury. A bear had been intruding upon some of his neighbors' farms and raising havoc in their corn fields. For some time it left Foster's farm and crops alone.

which made the neighbors believe that the bear knew Foster's character as a hunter, and so avoided his property. Finally bruin invaded Foster's orchard and feasted upon half ripe sweet apples he obtained by climbing the trees and clambering about among the branches, doing considerable damage by breaking the limbs. Foster watched his orchard late into the night, for several evenings, but the bear would not make his visits until he had given up the watch and gone to bed. Resolved upon other tactics, Foster set his huge bear trap at the entrance of the orchard but a short distance from his barn. Now the neighbors, one and all. waited anxiously to see if "Uncle Nat" would succeed in ridding them of this troublesome intruder upon the town.

For several nights the bear avoided the trap, but continued his depredations in the orchard. At last, one morning Mrs. Foster. who had gone to the farm yard to milk the cows. discovered bruin in the trap, and at once hastened to tell her husband, who was chopping wood at the house. He hurried in the house to procure his rifle. Just at this moment a neighbor arrived who was noted in the community for his brag and bluster. This man had repeatedly told how he would deal with the bear if only he had the opportunity.   He was there now to inquire if the bear had been caught.

Upon being informed that the animal was at that very moment in the trap down by the orchard, he manifested the greatest glee, and at once asked Foster for the privilege of shooting him.   Now Foster had little faith in his neighbor's ability to execute any kind of a beast under any circumstances because of his timidity, which the poor man always tried to conceal by boasting; but being always ready to please and accommodate a friend, he assented; but he took the precaution, after loading the rifle and giving it to his visitor, to sling over his shoulder his powder horn and place a couple of bullets between his fingers.

As they made their way to the orchard, the man was constantly telling him how he was going to give the bear a sure death by his unerring shot.   They went around the barn and came in sight of the bear, who was meditatively eyeing the paw that was embraced by the earnest jaws of the trap.   A glance told Foster that the animal was not very securely caught, only the tip of his paw and the claws being fast.   But he said nothing, resolving to have some fun with his boasting companion.   The bravado of his neighbor seemed to cool somewhat as they came in sight of the black monster, and he wanted to stop and take his "deadly" shot as soon as they had turned the corner of the barn. But Foster would not consent to this, insisting that they go much closer before he took his shot.

When they had come to a "close" distance, so close that it made the neighbor blanch with fear, Foster stopped and told his confident friend to shoot. He was a timid man, as we have said, and one thing he was really afraid of was a gun. He paused now to ask Foster if his rifle "kicked." Foster told him it might a little, but to go ahead and finish the bear. So he put the gun to his shoulder, took careful aim, then turned his head, shut both eyes, and jerked the trigger. Of course he pulled the sight off from the bear, and the bullet buried itself in the trunk of an inoffensive apple tree.

The shot had an effect on the bear for all that, for at the report of the rifle he gave a lunge and jerk which set him quite free, leaving his claws in the trap. As the smoke cleared away, the now thoroughly excited neighbor beheld the bear sitting beside the trap, sucking his in- jured paw.

This was enough to entirely unman him, and when the bear dropped upon all fours and made towards them, his fright was complete, and he frantically appealed to Foster, exclaiming, "Oh, Uncle Nat! Uncle Nat! What shall we do, what shall we do?"

Foster was too much amused to answer in words, but instead, he took the rifle from his demoralized friend, poured in a charge of powder, dropped in a ball and shot the bear in the heart.

The traps used to catch bears were ponderous things. Foster and Stoner each had one made especially for their use by village smiths. They weighed in the neighborhood of fifty pounds. It is needless to say that they were never "toted" very far into the wilderness, though Foster sometimes took his to Fulton Chain, after the road to Moose river was opened. The trap is now in the possession of one of his grandsons, as is also the powder horn and bullet pouch he carried in his tramps and hunts. The jaws of the trap are over two feet in length and five inches in width, and are armed underneath with ugly spikes. which penetrating the bear's foot, making escape impossible when once securely caught. The huge strap springs on each side which closed the jaws of the trap were reinforced by a second set of springs inside of the main ones.

To set this machine was no small task, nor was it by any means free from danger. It was almost impossible for one man alone to set it. The only way the double springs could be forced down was by placing the trap near the root of a tree, a log or rock, or some other object where a leverage could be obtained; then a stout and heavy stake or pole was placed across the spring with the butt of the lever under the log or stone, and one man by throwing his entire weight on the extreme end of the pole could force down the spring. He would then have to remain controlling the end of his lever while his companion went through the same performance with the other set of springs. At this juncture there should be a third man to set the pan. But when a third man was not at hand, they would succeed in adjusting it by one of them reaching and setting the catch. This was a risky thing to do, and the precaution was always taken by the man doing it of placing a billet of wood between the jaws before attempting to adjust the pan, lest the levers getting loose, he would find the horrible spikes piercing his own limbs. A chain some six feet in length, provided with two grappling hooks at the end completed the equipment of this ponderous apparatus.

The wolf traps used by the hunters were on

the same plan as this bear trap, but weighing only five or six pounds, and having only single springs on each side. The traps used in catching otter were also provided with two springs, only the whole trap was much lighter. For trapping mink, fisher and muskrat, traps with a single spring on one side was used.

Upon one occasion when he and his brother Shubael were following a line of wolf traps near Salisbury, they came to one in which a half-grown wolf was caught by one of its hind legs. At the approach of the hunters it crawled under a brush pile, snarling and growling at a great rate. For the fun of the thing, Foster resolved to take the snarler home alive. So he cut a forked stick and fixed a kind of halter about its muzzle and then released it from the trap and started with the captive for home.

The young wolf would go very quietly a little way, and then stop and spring at its captor. But it was easily controlled by the forked stick fastened to its nose. After getting it home he muzzled it and fastened it to a drag and allowed it partial liberty. It would roam about the place and into the house, much of the time keeping itself concealed under a bed. As it showed no signs of becoming domesticated it was finally slain, and the bounty obtained for its scalp.

Foster seemed to have a particular liking for strange pets. As we remember, while a lad he brought home bear cubs and panther kittens, and once captured a full-grown eagle. Later in life he continued the practice of endeavoring to make pets of the wild animals of the forests. He at one time had a full grown moose in his barn at Salisbury, which I have mentioned; this he captured one winter when the snow was deep and crusted. This moose became quite tame. The children of the neighborhood obtained great pleasure by going to Uncle Nat's, as they called him, and seeing his moose, petting it, and giving it handfuls of grain and other delicacies.

Foster's fondness for children was great. Under his rough exterior, as a hunter and trapper of animals of the wood and a slayer of Indians, he carried a most tender and warm heart, particularly for all children. He always had a kind word for them, with a lively regard for their childish delights. An incident has been related to me of a visit paid him by two sons of his brother Elisha, illustrative of this kind trait of his.

The boys were aged eight and ten, and had come to spend the day on Uncle Nat's farm. They found him busily engaged in chopping wood. But as soon as he saw the boys approaching him he ceased work and greeted them with a cheery "Hello, boys, glad to see you; come to spend the day with Uncle Nat? Well, now, you must have a good time." And with that he stuck his ax in the block and went around the farm with them, showing them the things that would interest them, all the while asking them questions of their own life; about their going to school; what chores they had to do at home, and similar questions. He took them to the pig sty to show them a hog he was fattening, which was already so fat it could hardly get up; took them to the barn to see the moose, and showed them his fish pond, promising to let them catch some trout from it after a while. Finally he asked the boys if they could shoot, but neither had ever fired off a gun, their father having long before abandoned the vocation of a hunter. So he told them he would show them how, and their eyes fairly glistened with pleasure at the prospect of Uncle Nat's teaching them to shoot.

Taking his young nephews to the house, he took down his rifle and explained it to them. They listened with awed attention, for Uncle Nat's reputation as a wonderful marksman and successful hunter was familiar to them. After explaining all the parts of the rifle to the boys,

and the manner of loading and firing, he took
them out to the wood pile to practice shooting,
the delighted boys leaping and running before
him. Arriving at the wood pile, Foster set up a
target a reasonable distance away by fastening
a piece of paper about the size of a silver dollar
to a block of wood. He then loaded the rifle
and gave the honor of the first shot to the oldest
lad, Aaron by name.

"Now, then," said he, by way of instruction,
"raise the sight until you've got in on the paper,
and then pull easy."

The rifle was heavy for Aaron, but he managed to level the barrel and fire, but did not even
hit the stump. His uncle did not discourage
him, however, but told the lad that he had done
"perty well," but that he could probably do a
"little better," and told the boys to watch the
paper while he fired.

In a few seconds he had loaded, and the boys
had hardly had time to fasten their eyes on the
paper before their uncle put a ball exactly
through its center. This quite astonished and
delighted them, and they capered about with
glee, shouting, "Do it again, Uncle Nat." But
he insisted that they all must take turns in
shooting, and so the younger lad took a shot;
and before they got through he had them so

they could hit a larger piece of paper by firing from a rest. In some such manner as this he entertained and amused the boys the whole day.

These side lights upon this phase of Foster's life show his true character. It was one of kindness and true integrity, and tends to enlighten the hardy and rough side of his life as a hunter, and the grewsomeness of its bloody conflicts with his dark-skinned fellow creatures.

Foster's exploits with Indians were always shrouded in a mystery. When a boy nothing was thought of shooting an Indian, but when he moved to New York and came to live in Herkimer county, the laws had become more strict and an Indian's life regarded of some value, so that when a person wantonly slew one, he was likely to be arrested and tried for it.

I believe that in spite of the fact that Foster had had instilled into his mind a hatred of the red man by his father, he never deliberately and in cold blood killed one. Yet when crossed by one, or threatened by any of them, he would shoot them without hesitancy, and as coolly as his father had done in his day, and as he had taught his son to do. Whenever Uncle Nat spoke of these experiences, however, he shrewdly made use of such guarded language, that no legal advantage could be taken of it.

Thus we see that in recounting his adventure with the Indians near Piesco Lake, from whom he rescued little Mary French, he did not say that he killed any of them. He simply said that he shot at the first Indian that was coming up the ravine where the girl, his dog and himself were concealed, and that the savage dropped his gun; that he fired again and the rear Indian turned and ran towards Piesco Lake, and then he fired that way. That was all. "The Indians," he declared, "may have all got back to Canada, but they did not molest him any more.'

In this way he told all his stories about killing Indians. They are all very brief and to the point. Here is one. He was telling some of his friends of the lucky shots he had made, and declared that the best shot he ever made brought him eighteen beaver pelts, a dozen otter skins, and twenty muskrat hides, together with several skins of mink. All of these he secured with the single discharge of his gun. This wonderful statement staggered the faith of even his best friends, who had the greatest confidence in his ability to shoot fast and quick and do destructive work with his rifle. One of them in the group to whom he was telling the yarn ventured to express a doubt about its truthfulness. Foster's simple reply to his skeptical friend was, "Wal, yes, it was a wonderful shot, but not so hard, either. I just had to take the filling out of a blanket to do it; that's all." No doubt of it. I haven't the slightest idea that the poor red skin who owned the pelts ever rolled himself in his blanket again.

One of his favorite expressions and mode of explanation whenever asked about any particular Indian he was suspected of making away with was, "Wal, the last I saw of 'em, his blanket was a smoking." Here is another one of his characteristic stories. "I was walking in the woods when I saw an Injun lay down to drink out of a brook; something was the matter with him, for he dropped his face into the water and drowned. I thought I might as well take his gun, blanket and stuff as to leave them there to spoil."

Another time he said that in one of his hunting excursions he fell in with an Indian who carried on his back thirteen otter skins; that he had no intention of harming the Indian, in fact did not know that he had killed him, but that he never let otter skins escape him alive. He fired, they all fell, and he picked them up and came away.

In the same guarded way he told of making away with the Indian Hess. As Simms in his book gives a very good account of this incident in the life of our hero, we will transcribe it from his work *verbatim.*

Before the American Revolution there dwelt about two miles from the present village (now a city) of Little Falls, an Indian named Hess, who took an active part in that conflict as a hireling of Britain, and who undoubtedly was one of the most cruel and bloodthirsty of his race. Some ten or twelve years after the war, this Indian returned to his former hunting grounds to prosecute his favorite avocation.

"A country inn at this period was, for the spread of knowledge to be smoked in and watered in, a kind of 'circulating medium;' a place where in the absence of our thousands of newspapers the people of the surrounding country met to learn news from *quid nuncs.* And as Little Falls * * * was then a place of some notoriety on account of her new inland locks and old moss clad rocks, the bar-room of the village tavern became the place where all the classic events of olden time, and all the improvements of the modern days were freely discussed.

"On a certain occasion Foster met the Indian Hess in the bar-room of the Little Falls tavern, and observing that his dress a-la-mode was that of a hunter, he attempted to engage him in conversation, but he feigned ignorance of the English language until his white competitor in beaver skins oiled his tongue at the bar, when lo! the seal on his lips was broken and he spoke English tolerably well. The two hunters soon after left the village and traveled some distance together, when the conversation turned upon Revolutionary days. Boasting of his individual exploits on the frontiers of New York, the Indian exhibited a tobacco pouch of delicate leather. 'This,' said the crafty warrior, 'me got in war. Me kill white woman, rip open belly, find papoose, skin him some, and make pouch.' Hess also opened the box in the breech of his rifle and exhibited some evidence he there carried of the number of scalps he had taken in the war. 'The tally,' said Foster afterwards, 'ran up to the almost incredible number of forty-five,' and he added, 'I had almost a notion to shoot him on the spot.'

"Just before parting the Indian inquired of his companion his name, and on hearing it he exclaimed, 'Ha, Nat Foster, you bad man, you kill Indians.'

"On the Indian making recognition of him, Foster thought he detected in his look and manner a 'lurking devil' that seemed to say, 'if ever you fall into my power you will feel it;' and hearing him call him an 'Indian killer' he believed the old Indian, if opportunity presented, would not scruple to take his life also. The boast of murdered innocence had drawn a frown across the sunburnt brow and stern features of the white hunter, that seemed to send back a defiance to the red man's look of meditated death. But they parted, and if not as friends, certainly not as avowed enemies. But each, no doubt, felt apprehensive that a second interview might not terminate so fortunately for both of them; and certain it is, that one of them at least resolved not to be over reached by the other.

"Not long after the above incident transpired, Foster was threading the forest alone in the northern part of Herkimer county, in the pursuit of game. In a secluded spot, far away from any regular trail, he came unexpectedly upon and shot a moose cow. While securing the noble game, its mate, a most ferocious bull, being attracted to the spot by the bellowing of the dam, attacked him with great fury. In a dodging fight the hunter was obliged to make some two or three shots in rapid succession. Foster reloaded his rifle before he ventured to approach even a fallen animal that had been so tenacious of life. He seldom changed his position in the woods without a charge in his gun. While advancing to the fallen bull he was startled to hear footsteps within a short distance, and was possibly not less surprised to find in the person of his new visitant the muscular form of the Indian Hess.

"Hess, supposing, as is presumed, that Foster's rifle was unloaded, now experienced no difficulty in 'murdering the king's English,' and at the end of a mighty whoop that told credibly for his lungs and the absence of balsams, shouted, 'Now Foster, me got you, me kill you now.' Between Hess and his intended victim there was a little marsh over which a tree had fallen. Mounting the log to approach the white hunter, he advanced with uplifted tomahawk and death boding mien, when the report of a rifle again echoed amid the fir tops of the forest, a bullet plowed its way through the Indian's heart, and with a guttural groan, the dark warrior fell dead upon the marsh. Lest Hess might not be unaccompanied in the forest, the eagle-eyed marksman hastily reloaded his rifle, and then quickly stamped the corpse of his victim deep into the soft mud of the marsh. Dark mystery hung over the fate of this lone hunter for years. Many remembered that his disappearance was sudden and unexpected; and others remembered that they had heard Foster say shortly after meeting him at Little Falls, that he had seen him once and only once after that.

"He confidently communicated many years after to Jacob S. Christman, with whom he was hunting, the fate of this unfortunate savage for whom—

> "No solemn bell's metallic tongue,
> E'er toll'd its death note on the breeze;
> Zephyrs alone his requiem rung,
> Where ivy green her mantle hung
> 'Mid plumed and bowing trees."

Thus does Simms beautifully close his description of the grewsome event, throwing the mantle of sentiment about the poor Indian's death. Would that we were all as kindly disposed and as gentle in our expressions.

Foster was not given up to any extent to the influence of sentiment. To him the shooting of an Indian under such circumstances was a grim necessity; there was no poetry about it for him. Nor did any scruple probably enter his mind at the taking of Indians' lives. And how could we expect it would? With his birth and his early years spent in a locality where the red man was regarded as a deadly foe, and whose introduction into New York State, and to the Adirondack wilderness was accomplished with stern

15

conflicts with still barbarous members of the race.

In the same way he regarded the trapping of game and shooting of deer. It was a matter of business with him; God had made the forests and put the wild animals there for his and others' use, and so he plied his trade as industriously as possible, even unto his old age, shooting his deer, bears and panthers, and trapping the smaller quadrupeds with zeal, thinning out the Indians whenever necessary; and though he sometimes displayed what would appear to many as an unjustifiable desire to slaughter game, yet it was because he regarded the business from a commercial standpoint.

Simms gives in his book, some accounts of a W. S. Benchley's association with Foster in a few of his hunts. This man and the famous hunter were once fishing from a boat on one f the Fulton Chain of lakes, when Foster discovered an old doe and two fawns feeding on the shore, about a quarter of a mile distant. The fawns were about as big as lambs at two months old. Foster was on fire in an instant. If he could kill the doe, he said, he could easily secure the fawns, and their runnets would bring him fifty cents each. Benchley remonstrated with him for wanting to kill the little fellows for so

small a gain, and proposed to pay him the dollar
and let them go. But no; that would not be
earning it, and nothing would satisfy him short
of a shot. His companion then refused to row
him within shot; one look, however, from Foster satisfied him that he might as well comply.
In doing so he however managed to make some
noise in the water to frighten the doe and her
fawns away, but not without strong expressions
of opinion from Foster that he did it intention-
ally.

The same person says that one time upon entering the Seventh lake with Foster, the eagle
eye of the latter discovered a buck feeding upon
a grassy beach nearly half a mile away.

Said Foster, "Benchley, put me ashore and I
will give you some venison for dinner."

Benchley did so, and then rowed out into the
lake far enough to see the deer. After watching
some time he saw Foster step stealthily from the
bushes upon the beach; at the same instant the
buck raised his head in alarm and the watcher
immediately saw the puff of smoke from Foster's
rifle, and the deer fell. At the hunter's call
Benchley rowed to him. he not knowing Benchley had seen him shoot or the deer fall.

"Well, Uncle Nat. said Benchley, "have you
killed him?" The old hunter straightened up

like a soldier, with his eyes flashing; grasping his rifle in his right hand and holding it aloft, he exclaimed, "Benchley, he never told a lie, when he speaks he tells the truth." His companion stepped ashore, and going to the carcass of the dead buck found he had put the ball precisely in the center of its forehead. "And considering," says Benchley, "that Foster was fully twenty-five rods from the animal and that he fired the instant it raised its head, it was an unusually good shot, even for him.' They dressed the carcass and as Foster had promised, they had venison for their dinner.

CHAPTER XII.

ONE time Foster's life was threatened by a pack of hungry wolves. The way he conducted himself on the occasion, and the manner in which he afterwards related the occurrence was characteristic of the man. It happened early in the spring, after he had been home for a short time and had returned to the wilderness for a final six weeks of trapping. On the third day in, he reached the beginning of his line of traps, at the intersection of the Lime Kiln creek and Moose river, where he camped for the night. His traps extended from here, up the creek to the lake of the same name. From there they ran north to Fourth Lake on the Fulton Chain, then taking a northeasterly course they extended as far as Racquet Lake.

The morning following his camp at the mouth of Lime Kiln creek, he started up the stream, visiting his traps as he went along. Although he did not expect to find much game in them, he visited them all for the purpose of setting and rebaiting those requiring it. As they lay on both sides of the stream he was constantly crossing from one side to the other on convenient logs and fallen trees, making slow progress up the stream. Not until he reached the falls on the creek, where he arrived in the middle of the afternoon, did he find game to amount to anything. Below and in the vicinity of the falls, he took from various traps and snares, three beavers, a fisher, one red fox, and several mink. This was better than he had expected, for beavers were usually caught by baiting the traps with fresh castereum or beaver caster obtained from the carcass of any beaver and setting the trap near the school or settlement of beavers. Minks were usually snared with the aid of a fresh decoy trail made by dragging the entrails and stomach of a deer or other large animal over the snow and setting dead falls and small steel traps baited with meat along the course. As he had not been on the ground for some time to attend to these details of the trapper's art, he was agreeably surprised to find so many of these animals taken.

Gathering all together, he carried them to a large flat rock at the foot of a hill opposite the falls, and set about the task of skinning the game, casting the flayed carcasses on the ground by his side. As it was late when he completed the

work he decided to camp where he was for the
night. With an eye to the speedy erection of a
shelter for himself, he selected the spot where
he had been working, and appropriated a side
of the rock that was perpendicular to rest the
roof of his hut upon; he quickly made a little
bower of boughs by placing poles from the rock
to the ground and covering them and closing
one side with the branches of evergreens. Then
cutting a huge armful of the evergreens he
strewed them on the ground underneath the little roof, and had a snug and well sheltered place
for the night. After gathering some firewood
he prepared his evening meal, which consisted
of a slice of corned venison toasted on a spit,
tea made in his tin teapot, and bread which he
had thus early in the trip.

While eating his supper he heard the dismal
howl of a wolf, as if calling another. Soon it
was answered by a responsive howl from one
deep in the woods, and this again was taken up
by another still deeper in the forest. Such
sounds were familiar to the lone hunter encamped by the rock, and he finished his repast,
lighted his pipe, and settled himself for a comfortable smoke, without givng heed to the dole-
ful sounds that came from the depths of the
woods; still the howls continued, increasing as

the darkness deepened. The wolves were evidently gathering in a pack for some purpose or another, but not thinking that they would disturb him, Foster finished his pipe with composure, and replenishing the fire, betook himself to his shelter, and wrapping his blanket about him, sought the sleep he desired and needed. At intervals of two or three minutes he would hear the long drawn out howl which would have sent terror to the heart of a person unused to such sounds, but which did not at all disturb our hero, who suffered himself to sink into a peaceful slumber, from which he was awakened in a couple of hours by the most startling noises that ever fell on a hunter's ears. His fire had burned low and the wolves had surrounded his camp in a pack, being attracted by the smell of the carcasses of the beavers and minks he had left by the rock. They were now having a furious fight over the meat, barking, yelling, squealing and snapping at each other in their eagerness to get the toothsome morsels.

For an instant Foster was frightened at the fearful din they were making and was puzzled as to how he was to escape from the predicament, for the pack had completely surrounded his camp, and were even crowded together in front of the opening of his hut. Seizing his rifle and ammunition he crawled out of his shelter and sprang for the rock, leaping over the ferocious brutes, who snapped at him as he cleared them.

The pack instantly surrounded the rock, and with howls and snarls they sat upon their haunches, licking their chops in expectation as they eyed the lone man hungrily, for the little meat afforded them by the carcasses of the beavers and minks, were nothing to a pack of wolves that had been enduring hunger a whole winter.

Once on the rock, Foster regained his composure and prepared to begin an onslaught on his foes by putting the usual six rifle balls between his fingers, and placing his powder horn within his easy and mechanical reach.

"I will say right here," said Foster, in after years, when he would relate the adventure, "it was not a very desirable place to be in, particularly if a man was anything of a coward, for the wolves were desperate and bound to have a square meal before they quit. But as captain of my own company, I determined to keep a cool head; I gave the word to assault the enemy and opened fire on the varmints, and if I ever made six shots in one minute I done it then, and though I couldn't see the sight of my gun I could see the outlines of the wolves by the light of the moon plain enough, and picked 'em off easy. At first they seemed inclined to stand their ground, and as fast as I could thin 'em out they would close up together like a lot of soldiers; but after a few rounds they began to weaken, and soon commenced to back off, and at last the retreat became general, and I was master of the field."

In fact, he had either killed, wounded or driven away the whole pack by his rapid and deadly firing. But with his usual indifference he descended from the rock and throwing more wood on the fire, sought his blanket again, not even looking out for the wolves he might have killed. He was not to remain long undisturbed, however, for he was awakened again in a couple of hours, by the wolves barking and yelping over a bone or possibly the body of one of their own number, down by the river. But as they were not threatening him, he rolled over for another nap, when he heard them approaching with ominous growls. Seizing his rifle he crawled out again, and stood his ground, this time in front of the rock. They were cowardly now, and kept outside of the feeble glare of light sent out by the glowing embers of his fire. He waited for them to come nearer, but as they kept back in the darkness, he fired at them at random.

"In a few moments," he declared, "all was as quiet as a grave yard;" and going back to his couch of boughs he rested quietly the remainder of the night.

The next morning he went out and inspected the field of battle, finding twelve dead wolves, and one wounded one some distance from the scene of the night's action, making thirteen in all. A number which he declared was unlucky generally, but was lucky for him on that occasion, as he succeeded in getting all the heads and pelts out of the woods, and ultimately collecting the large bounty due him.

Foster first visited Bald Mountain and the First Lake on Fulton Chain when a young man, and before any improvements had been made there. What is now so well known as the Old Forge did not exist. Brown or his son-in-law Herreshoff had not yet penetrated the wilderness, or probably even contemplated what was afterwards their vain attempt to subdue it, and cultivate the stubborn soil or wring from the heart of the mountains the valuable ores that are still believed by many to be there.

Fabulous stories are told of hunters finding extensive lodes of iron and lead, and it is sometimes hinted even more valuable ore. It is told of Foster that on one occasion when he was sojourning for some time on the Chain, a party of Indians invited him to join them in shooting at a mark, but that he declined on the ground that he could not afford to waste his bullets, for, although, he had the moulds for running bullets for his rifle he had no more lead. At this, it is said, one of the Indians volunteered to get him all the lead he wanted; taking his canoe the Indian paddled up First Lake, being gone a couple of hours. When he returned he had a lump of almost pure lead, as large as his head, which he declared he got from a "rock" in the woods; but its location he would not divulge. The truth of this story cannot be verified.

Another circumstance related of him, however, goes to show without doubt that Foster did find valuable ore or carbon in his wanderings in the wilderness. For he and his son David, who lived with him for a time at Old Forge, were aware of the existence of a vein —of valuable material of some kind. They never revealed its location, and after they withdrew from the wilderness, at the shooting of the Indian Drid, they abandoned, for a time at least, the idea of gaining any benefit from their knowledge. Finally Foster died, and his son David removed to Ohio. After a short residence there, he returned to New York with the express in-

tentions of making use of his knowledge of the
location of the vein in question; but before his
plans were matured he was injured by an ac-
cident. A stone fell on his limbs and crushed
them, from the effects of which he died. Before
his death, he dictated to his family a description of the trail to be followed from the Old
Forge to the vein, which was taken down in
writing by a member of his family. This docu-
ment which I have seen, is now in the possession of one of his kinsmen. But it would be
difficult, if not an almost impossible task, it
seems to me to make any use of it; as the
course is indicated by certain trees, stumps,
hillocks and rocks which must be quite changed
now. If this vein, which from the paper I would
take to be either lead or coal, and which a dying
man considered important enough to dictate
directions to, is ever found, it must be by renewed searches and developments.

But let us leave this "prospecting" feature into
which my story has drifted, and listen to an
adventure Foster had on this tract with a
couple of Indians, in which he disposed of them
in his usual way.

As I have said, when he was wont to first visit
the tract around the Old Forge and Fulton
Chain, it was still as wild and uninhabited as

in its most primitive days. It was destined however, to be the scene of activity and industry for a little while, then to relapse almost into a state of nature again, when it was to be the scene of the closing tragedy in the hunter's life, and finally to become the resort of thousands of sportsmen and others, seeking pleasure, recreation and health.

Foster first visited the part of the wilderness in July. Hunters often went into the woods at this time of the year to build their camps, as the bark of trees would peel readily only at this time. He "toted" in a great load of traps, and left them at Second Lake. He then proceeded to Fourth Lake, where he made himself a canoe. He then returned to Second Lake, getting his traps and scattering them along his contemplated winter's route, going as far as Long Lake. This task of distributing and concealing his traps being completed, he returned to Eighth Lake, where he built a substantial camp of logs and bark, located at the foot of the lake near the outlet. This he intended to use as his headquarters for the winter.

Hunters found it necessary as well as convenient to erect "way stations" or small camps along their routes, where they could store some wood for a quick fire, and have a convenient place to stop if night overtook them before they could return to their main camp. So after erecting the snug cabin on Eighth Lake, Foster rowed to the foot of First Lake, and looked about for a suitable place for locating one of these camps. Near the outlet of the lake he found what he recognized at once as a capital thing for a way station, and also a valuable place of concealment for whatever he wished to hide from roving Indians. It was the stump or stub of a huge hollow tree. The trunk of the tree had been broken off about seven feet from the ground, doubtless by some gale of wind. He cut a hole through the shell of the stump, and then cleaned and hewed out the rotten wood inside, so that he had a little room nearly six feet in diameter. By roofing the top with bark he had a tight and snug place of concealment for his things, and ample room for himself and his dog, if they were ever overtaken in those parts by a thunder storm, or had to spend the night there. Putting his pack basket on the bottom, he could seat himself thereon, and with his dog at his feet, could comfortably spend a few hours of repose in this strange hut.

Much pleased with the affair, he gathered some dry wood, and put it together with some traps, an axe, his tin teapot and frying pan in-

side, and closed the aperture he had made in the
side by drawing the bushes around it. Felling
a sapling so that its bushy top rested on the top
of the stump, thus effectually concealing the
bark roof. He concealed his boat by the shore,
and turned his face homeward, well satisfied
that he would find things as he had left them.
He returned the following November, and found
everything undisturbed; and commenced operation at once, setting traps on his route, operating
along the Fulton Chain, up the head waters to
Racquet Lake, and on to Long Lake, which
marked the end of his extensive course. It took
him a week to make the round. Then he returned to his camp on Eighth Lake, and "set up
housekeeping" in his cabin.

At first his success was far beyond his ex-
pectations; taking unusually large quantities of
fur, so that the outlook was for a season of the
most profitable trapping he had ever had. At
the end of a few weeks, however, the amount of
game he took from his traps grew constantly
less, the decrease being most prominent on the
northern part of his route. He found footprints
of Indians on this part of his line, and knew at
once that they were stealing from his traps.
They operated very cautiously, however, and he
saw nothing of them, or of the carcasses of the

animals they must have taken from his traps. They were so sly that he ceased attending to the upper end of his. route, and only operated between his camp at Eighth Lake and his stump camp at the foot of First Lake, for he knew that if he stopped setting and baiting his traps on the upper section of the route, the Indians, who were too lazy to either take traps into the woods, or attend to them even after they were placed, would then come down to the lower end of his route, and he would then have an opportunity to settle with them.

This plan worked as he expected. One forenoon he returned to his camp at Eighth Lake, having spent the night at his stump camp, and found the carcasses of several beavers and fishers by the camp. He examined them and found the marks of a trap on each one. This made him thoroughly mad; he was bringing traps from his home in Salisbury, toting them on his back some forty miles, and then the Indians getting the benefit. He resolved to "clean the Indians out," even if he had to "scare them clear to Canada" in doing it.

They were evidently in the vicinity now, and he determined to meet and "fix" them ere the sun went down. Fortune materially assisted him in carrying out this resolve, though he did not actually accomplish it until long after sunset.

Taking his rifle and getting into his canoe, he paddled swiftly, but cautiously, down the lakes, keeping a sharp lookout for the Indians. He went so far as Sixth Lake without seeing anything of them. At the foot of Sixth Lake he had to "carry," but undaunted he took his canoe on his shoulders, and quickly walked to Fifth Lake without a stop. Launching his craft here, he continued on his course to Fourth Lake, where he concluded to visit some of his traps to see if the Indians had visited them yet. Rowing into a little cove in the shore opposite Bear Island, he drew his canoe into some bushes that grew to the water's edge, and made his way to some mink traps he had set, quite a distance in the woods. He found them unmolested, some having game in them; this he took and returned to the lake. What was his surprise on reaching it to find a pack of furs, with some game, lying on the shore. He drew back into the bushes immediately upon discovering the heap, and peered cautiously around for those who had brought it.

Looking out upon the lake he was not surprised at seeing a canoe being paddled by two Indians towards the island. When they reached it they drew their canoe on the shore, and taking their rifles, disappeared in the woods that were then very dense on the island.

Foster now concluded that these Indians had left the fur and game where it was, to go and explore the island, expecting to find him encamped there. He had no doubt from their actions that they intended to shoot him if they found him there, and then return to get the things they had left, and continued their round of his traps. He examined the bodies of the mink and fisher that the Indians had left with the pack of furs, and found that they were still warm; and having the marks of the traps on their limbs, he knew that they had been but recently taken from his traps farther up the lake. The Indians were probably ashore when he rowed down, and did not see him, nor he them.

Fortunately he had taken pains to conceal his canoe when he landed, so that it escaped the Indians observation. Drawing it from the bushes, he hastily put the furs and all the game in it, and paddled rapidly down the lakes to his stump camp at the foot of Fourth Lake; when he arrived it was about four o'clock in the afternoon. The first thing he did was to start a fire, and cook himself some supper from provisions he had in the stump. After appeasing the hunger his long fast from morning had created, he began putting in operation a plan he had thought of for fooling the Indians. He knew they would soon return to the cove for the things they had left, and finding them gone, would probably conclude that he had visited the spot and taken them, and returned to his camp on Eighth Lake, of the existence of which he knew they must be aware. Thinking he had gone up the lakes, they would continue on down the lakes, robbing his traps as they went. When they reached the foot of First Lake, they would look about for a camp, and he resolved to have one ready for them.

Selecting a favorable spot a few rods from his stump, he proceeded to build one of those comfortable little huts of boughs he was so expert in making in so short a time. On completing the shelter he arranged a pile of hemlock twigs under it, and covered them with a blanket, so that it looked exactly like a figure of a man reposing. By the time he had completed all of these arrangements it was dusk; he now started a fire in front of the open end of the shanty, and betook himself to his hollow stump, and seating himself on his pack basket, with his dog at his feet, and his rifle between his knees, he waited to see what would come of his ruse.

As the darkness deepened the fire blazed more brightly, for he had put on a great quantity of wood. He watched its fierce burning with satisfaction, for he knew that if the Indians were in the vicinity they would see it, and as it burned low, and the night advanced they would investigate it. It was a weary vigil, and he allowed himself to fall into a doze, as he knew faithful old Watch would awaken him when the Indians came. He was a faithful canine, an exact counterpart of his mother Rose, who was the hunter's companion in his youth.

Foster had dozed and slept some time, when the dog roused him by his trembling body as it lay against his feet. He knew at once that Watch had scented the Indians. He cocked his rifle and peered out of the opening in the stump. The fire was now a heap of coals, which sent out a ruddy glow, just lighting up the interior of the hut of boughs, revealing the blanket as a sleeping man. His quick ear soon detected the careful dip of a paddle, and in a few moments he saw through the trees the two Indians in their canoe, appear from the inky darkness which hung over the waters of the lake; they paddled to the shore, stepped carefully out, and pulled their boats onto the beach.

They stood motionless on the shore for a

couple of minutes, with their rifles in their hands taking observations, and then began to pick their way carefully towards the camp.

Said Foster in relating this adventure: "As I watched 'em I got most excited as my dog, and could hardly keep from leaping out of my stump, and actually shooting 'em. The two red devils skulked along craning their necks, nodding their heads, and motioning to each other as they pointed to the fire and the hut. They would advance about three steps, and then they would stop and look and listen, and altogether acted like two of the most detestable and cowardly whelps that they were.

"Finally they got where they could see inside of the hut, and then the cusses had to stop and have another conflab with each other in their sign talk. I most made up my mind again to shoot 'em dead, they looked and acted so cussedly devilish, and I did get out of my stump and got up behind a big hemlock tree ready to shoot 'em; but I restrained msyelf and let 'em proceed. Finally they moved again, and worked up closer, so they had a good view of what they thought was me in the hut. Then, after a little more of their motioning, they both took aim at the blanket and fired.

"And this transaction" Foster was wont to

"They had a good view of what they thought was me in the hut."

say in concluding his account of the story, "so excited me that I yelled in my excitement, and my dog bayed with a vengeance, and sometimes I've thought," he would say in a reminiscent manner, "that I must have fired twice right in the direction of them Indians, but I was so excited I don't exactly remember. But anyhow, I know I discharged my gun, and I've always been of the opinion that it had the desired effect, for Watch and me didn't have any more trouble with the red devils after I scart 'em away from my stump camp, and I had a fine season of trapping."

This was Foster's first encounter with Indians on the Fulton Chain, and occurred several years before any white man had penetrated the wilderness to settle it. We see how easily he accounted then for the way in which he disposed of the Indians that troubled him.

Years after, however, he was to have an encounter with another one of the race, the serious outcome of which could not be easily gotten rid of.

CHAPTER XIII.

DURING the time intervening between the adventures with which the preceding chapter closes, and the tragedy narrated in the next, which is the closing event in the life of our hero, there were mighty changes wrought at that section of the Adirondack wilderness, where they occurred.

I am greatly indebted to C. E. Snyder, Esq., of Herkimer, N. Y., for much of my knowledge of the history of the tract where the closing tragedy of Foster's life occurred. Mr. Snyder recently prepared a paper on "Brown's Tract," which he read before the Historical Society of Herkimer County. He has given me the privilege, which I gladly avail myself of, of using his manuscript in my description of the development of the country where Foster hunted so many years; which development has such an important bearing on the closing scenes of his last days as a hunter and trapper.

In 1798, John Brown, a capitalist of Rhode Island, and a conspicuous patriot during the war of the Revolution, and afterwards a member of Congress, came into possession of the region known so many years as "Brown's Tract." He got it through the foreclosure of a second mortgage he held on the territory. It embraced 210,000 acres about the head waters of Moose River. It lay in the northern part of Herkimer, the western part of Hamilton, and the eastern part of Lewis Counties, and included the Fulton Chain of lakes.

These lakes received their name from Robert Fulton, the inventor of the steamboat. He explored the region in 1811, to ascertain the practicability of adopting the lakes and streams there, into the canal system which was then being developed by the legislature of the State. Fulton was very enthusiastic over the beautiful chain, and probably made reference to it in his first report to the Canal Commission, of which he was a member. At all events, from this time the lakes have been known as "the Fulton Chain."

After the close of the War of the Revolution, a large part of the territory of Northern New York passed through the hands of speculators, who inaugurated a land boom, which must have been something like the western land booms of recent years. But one man it appears made any money. That was William Constable, who bought 1,920,000 acres in 1792, and in the same year sold 1,280,000 acres, including what was afterwards Brown's Tract, to Samuel Ward of New York City, for one hundred thousand pounds. He doubled his money by the deal, and had 640,000 acres of his original purchase left. The ownership of this tract of 1,128,000 acres passed through several hands, until a part of it, what afterwards came into possession of Brown, was owned by Philip Livingston of New York City. A son-in-law of Brown's named Francis was responsible for the acquirement of the land by Brown, according to the statements of Mr. Snyder in his paper. He says:

"The story is told by the descendants of Brown's family, that a cargo of Indian merchandise had been landed and sold by Francis, who was an agent of Brown. Francis fell in with some land speculators, and yielding to the real estate boom then so universally prevalent, is said to have invested $50,000 of the money of John Brown in a second mortgage on Brown's Tract. This investment was from the start disapproved of by Brown, and was a source to him and his family of considerable loss.

"After Brown had acquired title to the land

upon the foreclosure of the Livingston mortgage, he began to take measures to develop and settle the country. He first caused a survey of the land to be made by Arnold Smith, Elkanah French and John Allen. The 210,000 acres were sub-divided into eight townships, which were numbered from one to eight consecutively, and also named. The names which Brown gave them are mottoes which are said to have been used by him in his business career. Township No. 1 was named Industry and was surveyed into 160 acre farms. Township No. 2 was named Enterprise and was surveyed into one-half mile squares. Township No. 3 was named Perseverance and was also surveyed into one-half mile squares. Township No. 4 was named Unanimity, Township No. 5 Frugality, Township No. 6 Sobriety, Township No. 7 Economy, Township No. 8 Regularity.

"After surveying the land Brown built a road through the forest from Remsen, Oneida county, to Township No. 7, upon his tract, a distance of about twenty-five miles. The road terminated near the south shore of the middle branch of Moose river in the center of the township, about two miles from the south boundary line of his tract, at which place he planned a settlement. The building of this road for a single individual must have been a great undertaking. * * Brown's aim was to make permanent settlements on the tract and to convert the wilderness into farms. A mill dam was built across the mouth of the middle branch of the Moose river, then called Mill creek, on the site of the present dam at Old Forge, for the purpose of obtaining power to run the sawmill and grist mill. The sawmill which he built is said to have been located in about the same place as the present sawmill at Old Forge. His grist mill is said to have been erected on the opposite side of the river, a little lower down the stream."

After the dam was built it was three months, it is said, before the water flowed over it, and a search was made supposing the water had found another outlet.

"Personally, Brown, so far as I can find," continues Mr. Snyder, "was only once upon the tract superintending its settlement. Its development was intrusted almost entirely to agents. Personally, Brown was a man of short stature and weighed in the neighborhood of three hundred pounds. He drove about in a specially constructed gig, built low so as to make it possible for him to get in and out. However, notwithstanding these physical defects, his descendants, I am informed, have recently discovered a letter showing that under all these personal disadvantages he made a visit to the tract.

"Brown did not long survive his attempted settlement; he died in 1803. How many settlers there were, and who they were and whence they came, is not known, so far as I have learned. The climate was cold and unfavorable for agricultural operations. The soil was poor, the location in the center of a large dreary forest, miles and miles away from any settlement. The tide of immigration was all towards the west, leaving this little community far to one side. Gradually the settlers whom he brought there left the place.

"By the will of John Brown the title to the larger part of Brown's Tract passed to his grandson, John Brown Francis, of Warwick, Rhode Island. Francis was at one time a Senator, representing his State in the United States Senate, and subsequently became its Governor.

Brown had another son-in-law named Charles F. Herreshoff, who became interested in the tract, through renewed attempts made by Francis to settle the tract after the war of 1812. He purchased a considerable part of Township No. 7, where he afterwards built his famous forge. He was a German by birth, and had a commanding appearance, being six feet tall, and very gentlemanly in his ways. It is also said that he was extremely proud and aristocratic, though this must be taken with consideration, for those from whom was received this verdict were the hardy settlers of the rural parts of the country who would not appreciate the retiring disposition and courteous bearing of a foreign gentleman. He was a finished scholar.

He went onto the tract in 1817 and spent the greater part of his time until his death, in the wilderness attempting to subdue and improve it. It is said that as he entered the forest for the first time he declared with an oath, that he would settle the tract or settle himself. Although less calculated than some men of smaller mental caliber to do the great work of settling a wilderness, still he accomplished considerable towards the fulfillment of his purpose. He repaired the mills Brown had erected, which had fallen into decay, and in the course of a few years had cleared up large tracts of his wild territory. Iron ore had been discovered during the old settlements, and iron works were projected by Herreshoff. At the site of the mills he erected a forge for the smelting of ore, and opened several roads from there to the settlements he scattered about on the tract.

Herreshoff is said to have manufactured exactly a ton of iron at his famous forge. It was of the very best quality, and cost, it is said, one dollar a pound. Black sand found on the lake shore and separated by magnets, was principally used in making this ton of iron. He expected to find ore in abundance in the mountains, but only succeeded in locating a small vein in some two hundred feet of rock, which he dug out at an enormous expense.

Mr. Snyder says of this attempt to obtain ore for smelting: "An iron mine was opened nearly opposite the site of the depot at Fulton Chain, and on the westerly side, where to this day is pointed out to the tourist a large hole in the rocks from which the ore was taken. Old drill marks are still to be seen about the mine at the entrance of which is a tree some eight inches in diameter, growing up among refuse thrown out of the mine; while at the bottom, fed by little veins of pure cold Adirondack water, is a well of some little depth. The place is sometimes spoken of as John Brown's well. * * * *

"There was no power near the mine to operate an iron works, or to reduce the ore, and Herreshoff accordingly built a mill, or forge, about one and a half miles away, near the dam across the middle branch of the Moose river, previously built by Brown, his father-in-law. His forge is said to have been located just below the grist mill. Heavy machinery was taken through the woods and set up here in the heart of the forest. Considerable preparation was made for manufacture of iron. A nail shop was started.

"Coal was, of course, necessary for the reduction of iron ore, and for this purpose charcoal was manufactured. *   *   *   *   *   *

"Herreshoff built for himself what must have been in those days and for that place, a fine house, made of timber and boards sawed at the old mill built by his father-in-law. The house was located nearly opposite the site of the railway depot at Fulton Chain, and on the westerly side, and subsequently became known as the Arnold house. It was standing until about a year ago (1895), in a dilapidated condition, when it was destroyed by fire. Herreshoff also built a large barn a short distance from his dwelling, on the top of which was a cupola in which a bell was placed for the purpose of summoning the men to their meals.

"Herreshoff struggled heroically," says Mr. Snyder, "against great odds. He planned for the conversion of the forest into farms and at the same time for the development of iron mines and iron works. The conditions for settling the country were, of course, just as unfavorable with Herreshoff as with Brown. The settlers whom

The old Herreshoff house, 1895

he brought upon the tract became discontented; poor soil, severe climate and isolation in the midst of a great forest, was more than Herreshoff could successfully contend with. Then he became indebted considerably to his miners and iron workers. The funds which he brought with him became exhausted. Drafts which he drew upon his family in Providence were returned unaccepted, and he was confronted with ruin."

I have learned from an old resident of the tract, that at about this time he began to brood much over his troubles, and was really suspected of losing his mind by his employees, and they rather expected that he would make away with himself. One day he ordered some of his men to the senseless task of filling up the great hole that had been dug in search of iron. They set about the work and continued it until Herreshoff went down into the pit and then ordered them to continue throwing in the rocks, logs and brush they were using to fill it with, when they decided he wished to commit suicide, and laid off from work that day.

Herreshoff is described by Simms as a good-feeling man in spite of his reserved ways and dignified bearing. "On one occasion," he says, "Herreshoff went with some of his men in a boat to the head of Fourth Lake, to select some

17

pine timber. Passing one of the islands of the lake, he desired to be set ashore on a bluff extending some distance into the lake.

"He was a great smoker, and having lit his pipe, he concluded to increase the fumigation by also lighting the grass and dry brush on the bluff about him. A few minutes only sufficed, with the breeze blowing, to spread the flames over the entire bluff. The wind drove the heat towards him, and calling for the boat to come to him, he gained the extreme point of land in hope of escaping the fire. Before the boat could get to him, however, the flames drove him out onto a tree which extended horizontally over the water.

"The craft seemed to him to move at a snail's pace, as the heat and smoke—of which latter commodity he for once had enough,—became more insufferable. He held on to his footing until he saw a sheet of flame coming along the trunk of the tree, and directly into his face, when he sprang off into the water, among the trout. He did not glide as noiselessly as they in that element, however, but floundered about like a porpoise, and for once, if we mistake not, quit smoking with tobacco still in his pipe; he was rescued by his employes, half drowned and half frozen, as he took the unexpected bath in September, and shivered for hours to pay for it."

The end came, however, in a short time; winter was upon him, and the great, ambitious man was no doubt keenly sensible of his utter helplessness. Cast down and burdened with despair, on the morning of the 19th of December, 1819, he went out to the northeastern corner of his house and sent a pistol ball crashing through his brain. A young woman named Hannah Merry, an employee of the house, was outside and looking up saw her employer fall to the ground. The report of the firearm brought other of his servants and attendants from the house, and David Sweet and Seth Lathrop, hired men, carried him into the house, where he soon expired.

"Such," says Simms, "was the melancholy and tragic fate of one of the most enterprising men that ever entered the wild lands of New York to subdue them."

The body of Herreshoff was carried to Russia Corners, a distance of fifty miles, where an inquest was held, after which the remains were taken to Boonville and interred in the village burying ground. When the present cemetery of the town was laid out, his body was taken up with others in the old burial plot and interred in the new one, where it is now, marked by an old-fashioned slab of marble which his relations caused to be erected at his grave a few years after his death. It bears the simple inscription of "Charles Frederick Herreshoff, Obiit Dec. 19th, 1819. Aetat 50."

With the death of Herreshoff his settlements became tenantless, and remained so with exceptions of two or three renewed attempts made from time to time by different families to live on some of the clearings. But they were generally deserted, being only visited by hunters who camped in the deserted dwellings. Those clearings about the foot of the chain were the ones occupied by tenants longest. Otis Arnold was the last one to occupy the old Herreshoff house and farm it for a living. He rented the place soon after Foster got into trouble by shooting the Indian at Indian Point in 1833, and remained there many years. He grew large crops of oats. and threshing them in the fall, would draw the grain to market in the winter; about the only time loads could be taken over the road, which had fallen into decay.

Of this period of the history of the tract Mr. Snyder says: "Many accounts are to be met with of visits to Arnold's, during this period, all of which are entertaining. In the autumn of 1855, the Honorable Amelia M. Murray, maid of honor to Queen Victoria, went over the lake belt of the wilderness with Governor Seymour, the Governor's nieces and other friends. On their way out they stopped at Arnold's, and the story of the diary of Lady Amelia is in these words: 'Mr. Seymour remained to make arrangements with the guide, while his niece and I walked on to Arnold's farm; there we found Mrs. Arnold and six daughters. These girls, aged from twelve to twenty, were placed in a row against the wall of the shanty, with looks so expressive of astonishment, that I felt puzzled to account for their manner, until their mother informed us that they had never before seen another woman than herself. I could not elicit a word from them, but at last when I begged for a little milk, the eldest went and brought me a glass. I then remembered that we had met a single hunter, rowing on Moose river, who called out, 'Where on earth did them women come from.' "

"Another tourist, Wallace, in his 'Babes in the Woods,' gives this account of a visit to Arnold's: "As we approached the house we passed through a yard where the daughters of the family were engaged in milking, with a little smoking fire beneath every cow. Here was a new feature. Such remarks as the following greeted the ears of the milkers: "If they are not smoking their beef with the skins on!' 'I have heard of building fires under balky horses, but I fail to see the necessity of serving cows that way.' 'Boys, can't you see,' said another, 'that this is done as a matter of domestic economy. The gradual and increased warmth acts upon the udder of the animal and through this upon the lacteal contents thereof, producing a sort of coagulation whereby the creamy globules are precipitated.' By this time we had begun to learn by experience that the smouldering fires were smudges to drive the punkies from the cows so that they might be milked in peace." "Here, perhaps, is another reason," says Mr. Snyder, "why the Brown and Herreshoff settlements proved disastrous. Unless they knew how to manage punkies, they certainly did a wise thing in moving away."

But let me return to the period when Foster occupied the house as a tenant. In May, 1830, the premises were leased by Caleb Lyons as agent of the Browns, to David and Solomon Maybee, for thirty dollars. Two years later, Feb., 1832, Foster, who had traversed the region as a hunter during all the vain attempts to settle it, purchased an assignment of the lease for ten dollars and moved his family there, that he might with greater convenience follow in his old age his favorite avocation of a wilderness trapper and hunter. He intended, no doubt, to spend the remainder of his days there among the mountains and lakes he loved, and to thread the forests in pursuit of noble game. But he was destined to spend but a few years there, however, and that, harassed and rendered unsafe by a lazy, but treachrous Indian, who made himself at home on the tract. It seems as if the Indians were to be forever his foes, and that even in his old age, he must administer some of his stern discipline to intrusive red men.

WHEN Foster took up what he intended, no doubt, should be his permanent residence on Fulton Chain in 1832, he was over sixty-five years of age. He rented the farm at Salisbury to his son Amos, and took his wife with him into the wilderness. They occupied as their home the Herreshoff house. In a short time they were joined by their son David, accompanied by his wife and child. The Fosters were the only white families on the clearings at the time, though three old bachelors lived in another one of the abandoned dwellings situated on the "Middle Clearing," being about half way between the Herreshoff house and the dam. It afterwards became knows as the Slocum place. The names of the three men were William S. Wood, David Chase and Willard Johnson. The latter had gone into the woods to work in the forge at his trade as smelter, but upon the abandonment of the works he continued there, hunting and trapping for a living, and was joined by Wood and Chase in his hermitage.

"He threw up his arms in terror at the moment of explosion."

In a rude hut or shanty not far from their
dwelling, lived an Indian named Peter Waters,
but familiarly known in the forests by the name
of Drid. He was a quarrelsome fellow, and as
soon as Foster settled on the tract, began to
use every conceivable means to pick a quarrel
with him. No doubt the fact that Foster was
known as a man who had slain many of his race
and bore the reputation of an Indian killer, intensified his hatred of the old hunter. And from
the fact that he was now advanced in years and
his fighting days were practically over, Drid er-
roneously thought he could treat him with the
insolence and audacity he did; but he "reckoned
without his host," for the old man had not "lost
his cunning," nor "his hand its skill," as the
reckless warrior was to discover in due time.

Foster, during his residence at the Chain, was
very jealous of his rights there. He had leased
the tract for the express purpose of hunting and
trapping undisturbed during the last years of his
life. W. S. Benchley, writing of him in 1843,
says: "I spent several days upon the lakes with
Foster at this time. He conversed but little,
and his restless, roving eye was never still. With
his rifle at his side, he seemed ever anxious to
discover something on shore worthy of his unerring aim. Frequently he would direct my at-

tention to an object on some distant grassy
beach, saying, 'See, there is a deer; watch and
you will see it move.'   He was never mistaken.
Still, one less accustomed with the woods would
very seldom have supposed that anything of the
kind was in sight.   The bald eagle, which is
frequently seen in this region," continues Benchley, "Foster would never disturb, for he thought
those noble birds were made to live unmolested
by man, although he said, 'the cussed Injuns
shot them.'"   His sentiments appear to have
undergone a change in this respect since his boyhood, or perhaps the memory of Old Put caused
him to entertain a sentimental regard for the
noble bird.   "He seemed to feel as though he
was lord of the tract," says Benchley, "and no
one else, especially an Indian, had as good a
right there as he."

The same writer says: "Along the northern
shore of Second Lake rises a most grand and
sublime mountain (Bald Mountain) presenting
the front of a naked rock for nearly a mile, at a
height of several hundred feet.   On its summit
Uncle Nat told me he had often been, and that
from that elevated position he could see the
lakes for miles around, and that there he could
enjoy himself 'and not be troubled by the d——d
Indians, especially that black devil, who was all

the while threatening his life.'" The Indian al-
luded to is said to have been quite successful
in killing deer, and often "floated" for them.
This mode of securing the noble game much
displeased Foster and it is believed to have been
one source of difficulty between them.

The real trouble between Foster and the Indian began soon after the former took up his
residence on the tract. Drid took Foster's boat
from its moorings at the dam without his knowledge or consent, and left it a mile up the river.
As soon as Foster missed his boat he looked up
the Indian and compelled him, at the muzzle of
his rifle, to lead him to the spot where he had
left it. He found the Indian had stove a hole
in it, and as he was bending over examining it,
Drid jumped on the old man and attempted to
knife him. In spite of his age Foster threw
him off and cocking his rifle told Drid to "Be-
gone before I shoot you in your tracks." Seeing the flash of the old man's eye, he slunk sul-
lenly away, and from that time until his death,
he constantly threatened the hunter's life, and
made several unsuccessful attempts to shoot or
tomahawk him.

The Fosters were always kind to the Indian's
family, and when he was away on a long hunt,
his squaw depended almost entirely on this kind-

ness for the support of herself and children. This was continued after the quarrel the same as before. Foster kept a cow and the family of his Indian neighbor, as well as the white residents, were supplied with milk free of charge. But such articles as Foster had to bring into the woods, he would make a charge for. On one occasion when he very civilly asked the Indian to settle the account he became very abusive and made a positive threat against the life of his kind-hearted old neighbor.

"In July, about two months before his death," says Simms, "Drid was returning from a hunt in company with a white hunter named Carpenter, who frequented the tract. As they drew near the upper clearing the Indian discharged his rifle and reloaded and carefully primed it. His companion inquired why he did it, saying he would not find game so near the clearing. 'Me going to shoot ole Foster,' answered Drid, and he did go to the Foster dwelling, and standing some distance from the door, he hailed several times to draw Foster, if he was in the house, to an exposed situation. The halloo was answered by Mrs. Foster, who was alarmed when she saw the threatening attitude of her dusky neighbor. He inquired for her husband, and being told he was not at home, he exclaimed as he turned to go, 'Me shoot him if he had been.'"

The next morning the family of Drid being out of provisions, applied, as usual, to the Fosters for food. Being informed by his wife and Carpenter of the Indian's conduct of the night before, Foster took some flour and, accompanied by Carpenter, sought the red man's shanty to relieve the wants of his family and to question him in regards to his conduct the previous night. In the presence of the witness he asked Drid if he had not called at his door the night before, intending to shoot him. The Indian readily admitted that he had, and assigned as a reason that he had threatened to kill him. 'I made no such threat,' said the old man, warmly; 'I simply said that it wouldn't be well for you to take my boat again and leave it a mile from the dam with a hole in her bottom.'"

Sometime after the above incident, the Indian was at the Foster dwelling with one or two of the neighbors, when the old trapper again asked him to pay his account. The Indian instantly flew into a passion, exclaiming, "You a d——d liar, me don't owe you a cent," and raised his tomahawk to strike the old man, who quickly sprang into his house, and reappeared instantly with his rifle in his hand, when his foe slunk back and exclaimed, "Foster, if ever you go to

Eighth Lake, me kill you," and with many threats he went to his cabin.

Realizing that what was once his privilege in the woods, would not be tolerated now by law, Foster soon after the above occurrence, went to Justice of the Peace Joshua Harris, of Brantingham, twenty miles away, to swear out a peace warrant against the Indian; but the officer declined to issue one, saying that the Indian would be as likely to kill him if he did, as he was now to kill Foster. It seems that Drid was well known to the people in that part of Lewis county, and I have ascertained that he frequently tramped out of the woods to the settlements for bartering and trading. The Justice advised Foster to remove himself and family from the forest.

"What!" exclaimed Foster, "after I've hunted the red devils there over thirty years, be scared away by one? If you won't give me protection, then I'll protect myself;" and with this decision he returned to the tract and continued his hunting and trapping.

The little community of twelve or fifteen souls, composed of the Fosters, the three bachelors and the Indian's family, was occasionally visited by men who came to spend a few days or a week in hunting and fishing. They were generally residents of the towns on the borders of the

wilderness in Oneida and Lewis counties. Par-
ties of half a dozen men would come from Low-
ville or Boonville, spend the night with Foster,
and make arrangements with him or his son to
act as guide up the lakes. The bachelors also
acted as guides to the visitors who occasionally
came in. This may be regarded as the beginning of the present extensive excursions and
trips to the Adirondacks, made by thousands
every summer. It was also, I believe, the beginning of the extensive system of guiding now
maintained by a noble lot of fellows, as a whole,
who make it their entire business the greater
part of the year, to guide and assist the visitors
about through the net work of trails that now
girdle the entire wilderness.

The journey into the wilderness, too, has been
facilitated in recent years by the construction of
the Adirondack and St. Lawrence, and Mohawk
and Malone railways, whereby one may quickly
and comfortably reach the heart of the mountain and lake region to enjoy the superb scenery,
the invigorating atmosphere, and restful stillness
of the grand and mighty district.

If he chooses, he may angle for the saucy
trout, or hunt, at the proper season, for deer;
and yet, if not successful in either diversion, he
should still be well satisfied and repaid by rea-

son of his simple presence in that grand park
of nature, which has successfully resisted, thus
far, the vandal hand of man. It is to be hoped
that the lawmakers of the State will take steps
to properly protect and preserve it, both from
destructive speculations in its wealth of timber,
and from monopoly in ownership and control of
its beautiful rivers and lakes, and boundless ex-
panse of forests which should be kept open for
use by all who wish to properly use the great
park for rest and recreation.

Early in the month of September, 1833, four
men in the town of Leyden, then on the edge
of the wilderness, arranged to go to Fulton
Chain on a salmon fishing trip. The party consisted of Jonathan Tyler, and his son Willis,
Herman Thomas and Nelson Stimpson. They
started for the chain on foot the morning of the
16th, and arrived at the old Herreshoff house
in the afternoon. Foster was at home and gave
them a hearty welcome. One or two of the
party were well acquainted with him, while one,
Mr. Stimpson, had never met him before,
though, of course, thoroughly familiar with his
name and reputation as a hunter and trapper.
Mr. Stimpson, who is still living in the town of
Leyden at the advanced age of ninety-three (1897)
gives his first impression of the old hunter as

most pleasant and favorable. He made them feel at home at once, and showed them about, explaining the interesting places in the clearing to those who were not familiar with them. He exhibited to the party several specimen proofs he had of his successful following of the chase. He had a large and varied collection of deers' antlers and many finely cured skins of wild animals. It is evident that he became an expert taxidermist in the course of his life; besides these skins, which he showed the visitors, he had the mounted skins of four panthers set up, on a row of ash barrels by the house. They appeared, Mr. Stimson says, "as natural as life." Foster showed these specimens with pride, for they bore the mark of his bullets which had brought them to their death. "And each one," Mr. Stimpson declares, "had been shot right in the center of the forehead."

When Foster learned that the party came for salmon fishing, he volunteered to accompany them up the lakes the next morning, which offer was gladly accepted, as he could show them the best places for casting. The old hunter entertained them during the evening with reminiscences of his life and adventures. The stories he told, the reader is familiar with as being already given in other parts of this book. Indeed,

18

I was much surprised and pleased when I came to interview Mr. Stimpson, to have many of the adventures of Foster I had already obtained from various sources, retold to me by him, and without my interrogation, as stories told him and his party by Foster himself at this time. Thus, "in the mouths of two or three witnesses," they are established.

The night before the eventful day on which Foster shot Drid, was the one the fishing party arrived on the tract. Among other adventures which Foster related were several of the Indian stories I have given, which he told in his usual guarded manner, so as not to incriminate himself. The conversation drifted to the subject of Indians in general, however, and then Foster told them that there was one "red devil" on the tract at the time who was giving him a great deal of trouble, and that "if he could catch him out anywhere he would put him where the dogs wouldn't bite him." No one of the party doubted but that he would do this, though they little thought they would see him do it. There is no doubt but that Foster had decided to kill the Indian Drid, having failed to get a precept from the law against him. But it is doubtful if he intended to shoot him in as open a manner as he did the next day, although he was convinced that

he had to meet and settle with the enemy somewhere, as he had been compelled before to shoot
many another Indian in the depths of the forest
where no eye of man would observe his slaying
his enemy, and about which there would be no
questions asked when the savage did not appear
at his usual haunts. But he failed to follow this
usual course, and instead, shot his foe on the
principal waterway of the tract, and when there
were many witnesses of the deed. This brought
him for the first time into serious conflict with
the law, and brought about his only indictment
and trial for killing an Indian.

The men of the fishing party retired late, but
arose early in order to get an early start. After
breakfasting they started, accompanied by Foster. When they arrived at the middle clearing,
he asked the party to stop while he would inquire if Wood and Chase were ready, as he knew
they were going up the lakes that morning, and
he thought they might all go together. So they
paused outside of the bachelors' lodge, setting
their packs down for a rest while he entered the
domicile. He found the bachelors eating their
breakfast, while seated on the wood box by the
fireplace, smoking his pipe, was his hated enemy
Drid. He had some traps which he wished to
get at Raquet Lake, and had invited himself to

accompany Wood and Chase as far as they went.
Foster took no notice of him, however, but entered into conversation with the others about
the fishing party outside, and inquired when they
would be ready to start. Wood told him in
about an hour or possibly less, and Foster turned
to go, when the Indian started up and blurted
out, "Foster, you old cuss, what for you call me
rascal the other day?" Foster thinking to turn
the question away, answered in a jocular manner, "Because I was a mind to;" but this appeared to only inflame the Indian to action, and
he sprang upon Foster. He was a lithe, muscular
fellow, and only about twenty-five years old, but
in spite of this advantage, he could not master
the old man who clinched him. The bystanders
quickly separated them, Drid calling loudly for
his tomahawk, and Foster for his rifle; he was
excited by this time, and as he regained his feet,
he exclaimed, "You want to pick a quarrel with
me this morning, you black — — — —?" when
the Indian, who had shaken off those who had
pulled him away, sprang at the old man, this
time with his knife drawn. His quick and unexpected attack took Foster by surprise, and he
was borne to the floor by the Indian, who was
just about to plunge his knife into the old man's
heart, when Wood struck his hand, and the

knife inflicted only a flesh wound on Foster's wrist. Again the Indian was seized and pulled away, swearing like a pirate, exclaiming at the end of a horrid oath, "Foster, you old cuss, you no live till Christmas;" and Foster, whose worst passion was aroused, retorted, "and you'll do d——d well if you live to see another moon."

He now joined the waiting and anxious fishermen, who had been alarmed, as well they might be, by the tussles and loud talking going on in the house. He procured some cloth from one of them and bound up his wrist, telling them they must go on without him, as he would not think of going up the lake that day. Leaving them, he started towards his own home. They watched him until he was hid from view by the trees, when they gathered up their things and started for the dam. They had gone but a few rods, however, when the report of a rifle up the road startled them. It was evidently fired by Foster, and they wondered if he had seen a deer to shoot. It was Foster's rifle they heard, but it was not a deer that caused the old hunter to discharge his piece. He had simply rid it of its present charge, to carefully load it for game of another kind.

His mind was thoroughly settled. He must shoot the Indian ere he returned from his trip up the lakes or he would shoot him, or possibly murder him in his bed; for the Indian had threatened several times to enter Foster's dwelling in the night and stab him as he was sleeping. He now loaded his trusty rifle with two balls, and making a detour through the woods, he came out on the road ahead of the fishermen. When he reached the dam, he crossed to the north side of the river, and made his way through the forests to a point on the river, just below First Lake, where the boats, as they came up, had to pass. Taking up a position on this point among some bushes and between two large hemlocks, he awaited the arrival of the party.

The fishermen reached the dam without incident, and there waited for the arrival of Wood and Chase for instructions as to what boat to take. In due time they arrived, accompanied by Drid, who was still swearing vengeance at Foster, and was half inclined to abandon his trip to Racquet Lake and return to Foster's house to shoot him. He was dissuaded from this course, however, by Wood and Chase, who prevailed on him to accompany them, and by doing this, instead of preserving, as they thought, the safety of Foster, they only lured the Indian to his own death. After some delay in getting ready they all left the dam, Drid in a light bark canoe, Wood and Chase in a large bark canoe, and the fishing party in a wooden boat.

It is a twenty minutes' row from the dam at the Old Forge to Indian Point. At length the little fleet of boats drew near. Wood and Chase had some traps on shore here, and they and the Indian ceased paddling to put in and get them, while the fishing party continued on up the stream. As they neared the point, Mr. Stimpson, who sat in the stern of the skiff, espied Foster standing bareheaded among the bushes on the extreme end of the point, his rifle in his hand. Though surprised at seeing him there, when he had apparently gone home an hour before, Stimpson knew at once what he was there for, and apprised the other occupants of the boat of the old hunter's presence on the point. Instantly aware of the tragedy that was to be enacted, the rowers nervously but quickly pulled the boat past the point, while all excitedly awaited the event. As they rounded the point, Stimpson turned in his seat in the stern of the boat, and motioning to Wood and Chase, pointed to the shore, and they, too, as they paddled to the shore, saw Foster farther out at the point. Knowing what object brought him there they got their traps without a moment's delay and pushed out into the stream.

The Indian now guessed from the actions of the members of the fishing party and the conduct of Wood and Chase, as they hastily got their traps, that the man he feared was on the point, and he changed the position of his canoe so that it was on the south side of the trappers' canoe, and his own body midway between theirs.

"Although Foster was several rods distant from the canoes," says Simms, "still the position of his ioe did not secure his safety. As they rounded the point the Indian's eye caught a glimpse of the fearful figure in the bushes just as the rifle was poised, and he threw up his arms in terror, at the moment of the explosion. Both bullets entered his left side near the arm-pit, passed through his heart and went out below the right arm. They entered at the same spot, but left two places of egress opposite. The Indian fell backwards, with his head and shoulders in the water, his feet and legs remaining in the canoe. He fell so dead that his position remained unchanged, the fairy craft preserving the cradling motion communicated to it by the fall, for some time after the spirit of its owner had winged its flight."

To range the circuit of the sky.

Wood and Chase, who really saw the shooting, and the members of the fishing party who, from

their position on the river beyond the point, only
heard the report of the rifle, but knew its sig-
nificance, were, according to their own testimony at the trial, "perty badly frightened," so
much so that one of the fishing party did not
visit the chain again in ten years.

As soon as the echoes from the old hunter's
rifle, which had brought down its last Indian,
had died away, Wood and Chase set up a great
hallooing to the fishing party to come back, as
there was a dead man in the river. They obeyed,
though reluctantly, for they did not wish to be
mixed up in the affair; for as Mr. Stimpson expressed it, "it was going to spoil our fishing
trip." When they arrived at the scene Foster
had disappeared, and Wood and Chase were
ashore. They, anxious to free themselves from
any future complications, now discharged their
guns to show the fishermen that they had not
fired the shot that brought death to Drid. They
then had a consultation, as to the disposition of
the Indian's body. Some said it ought not to
be disturbed until it was viewed by a coroner;
while others pronounced this as absurd, as it
would take at least two days to notify a coroner
and get him onto the tract, during which time
the body would become loosened from the canoe
and float away. They were not able to arrive at

an agreement, and so returned to the dam, and concluded to do what was a little ironical; that was, to ask Foster's advice.

Wood and young Tyler went to his house for this purpose, leaving the rest at the dam. The distance from the point where the shooting occurred to the dam is greater by water than a direct route on land, and Foster, having traversed the land route, returned home before the others had returned to the dam. He had wiped out his rifle and changed his clothes ere the messengers arrived. Some say he shot a deer on the way home and had it dressed and hanging in front of his house when they arrived. But I have not been able to verify this statement. They found the old man resting on a bed; he had on his best suit of clothes and a linen shirt with an old-fashioned starched collar. He appeared to have made himself ready for going out of the woods at once. He expressed surprise at seeing Wood and Tyler, and inquired what brought them back. They replied that Drid was dead up the river and they did not know what to do about getting the body down, and had come to ask his advice what to do. The old man expressed no surprise at the announcement of the Indian's death; but did so at their being afraid to touch the body. He told them they should have no hesitancy about getting it to the landing, and offered to go with them and assist. The messengers agreed to this and he arose and accompanied them to the dam.

When they arrived, all but Stimpson and the elder Tyler embarked in the skiff the fishing party had used, and with Foster in the stern steering they rowed to the scene of the shooting. They found the body still floating as it fell, with the legs in the canoe. Even then all but Foster declined to touch it, and so, while the others held the canoe, he got the corpse back into it, and they then towed it to the dam, where the tiny craft with its gory cargo was made fast to the landing, and a blanket procured and thrown over it. The matter of notifying a coroner and justice was then talked over with Foster and they all agreed to go out the next day.

The fishing party, to whom the events of the day had brought an abrupt ending of their plans, again stayed with Foster over night, and he entertained them as on the previous evening with stories of his adventures in the woods.

One of the striking things to be noted in connection with the conduct of all after the tragedy, is, that no mention was made by any one, of how Drid came to his death. Foster neither feigned ignorance or intimated the least knowledge of

it. He followed the course any attorney would
have told him to, and set the seal of silence on
his lips. The next day all tramped out of the
woods, Foster being in as jovial and good-na-
tured a mood as any, telling them, as they passed
a ledge of rocks, of how he had shot a panther
and deer there. The house of the first officer
of the law they reached after an eighteen mile
tramp was that of Justice Harris, who had refused a few months before to issue a peace warrant to Foster against the Indian he had now
slain. They found Harris at home and the witnesses related the affair to him and asked him
to issue a warrant for Foster's arrest. But to his
credit be it said, that though he had shown his
weakness of character in not granting a peace
warrant to Foster against the Indian, now showed
his friendship for Foster by refusing to cause his
arrest, referring them to a justice who lived a
few miles farther, and had Foster stay with him.
The rest of the party continued on their journey
until they came to the home of Justice Lyman
R. Lyon, to whom Harris had referred them.
But he, too, declined to issue a warrant for the
old hunter, who was a friend of his, and referred
them to still another justice, Segar, in the town
of Turin. They found Justice Segar, afterwards
a judge, at home. After hearing the facts of the

case he issued a warrant for Foster and detained
the whole party over night at the public house
as witnesses. In the morning he dispatched a
constable to the home of Harris to arrest Foster. The officer returned about noon with his
prisoner, who came willingly, and cheerfully
submitted to the examination. Court was convened in the sitting room of the tavern, and after
the witnesses had been sworn and testified, Foster was remanded to jail in the village of Mar-
tinsburg.

It is presumed that a coroner was sent to the
Old Forge and viewed the remains of the Indian and then buried them, though I have been
unable to ascertain as to this. Simms says in
his book that the body was buried the day of
the shooting and that Foster assisted. But Mr.
Stimpson declares that the body was left in the
canoe, covered with a blanket; and it must have
been buried by the coroner, or under his direction, by either Willard Johnson or Foster's son
David, who were the only men left on the tract
when the others went out. A brother of Drid
came to the Forge from Canada soon after the
shooting. They belonged to the St. Regis tribe.
He took up his brother's body and reinterred it
in Indian style. Drid's squaw, it is said, manifested no emotion at her husband's death, and

the nearest approach she showed to any interest
in his body, was to cut out the pieces of blanket
which contained the bullet holes for keepsakes,
when the reinterrment took place. Her brother-
in-law took her and her children, of which she
had a number, back to Canada with him. The
grave of this last Indian Foster shot was to be
seen near the shore at Old Forge for many
years. The mound was marked by a cross bearing the simple inscription of "Pete." In recent
years it has been neglected, and when I visited
Old Forge in 1895 I found it covered with a pile
of lumber, the product of the sawmill still maintained there. If restored and marked it would
be an interesting feature of the place.

Times had changed. The law had penetrated
even to the heart of the Adirondack wilderness.
Foster was well aware of this, as we can see by
his long toleration of the Indian's insolent conduct. Foster did not remain long in the Mar-
tinsburg jail. The shooting occurred in Herkimer county, and so his friends in Salisbury,
to the number of one hundred, went to Martins-
burg and took him to the Herkimer county jail,
in the village of Herkimer, where he remained
until his trial. He was indicted for murder at a
court of General Sessions convened in Herkimer
on February 3d, 1834. He was arraigned for

trial September 3d, of the same year, in the Circuit Court of the county. Although the trial lasted but two days, it attracted great attention, for Foster was very popular all through that part of the county. The account of the trial as given in Simms' book is quite interesting. The prosecution had first to prove that Foster really fired the shot which brought death to the Indian. This was not actually proven by direct evidence, so skilfully did the defense cross-examine the witnesses presented by the people. Neither Wood or Chase or any member of the fishing party were able to swear that they saw the discharge of Foster's rifle, though all had seen him on the point, immediately before the Indian was killed. They all heard a shot and Wood and Chase saw the Indian fall, but no one saw Foster shoot. From this the attorney for the defense very suavely argued that the Indian might have been killed by a stray shot from a hunter in the woods. For the defense it was an easy matter to present evidence to prove the quarrelsome disposition of the Indian. Any number of hunters and others were in the court room ready and willing to testify to this. Next, the threats and attacks the Indian had made on Foster's life, particularly the one of the morning he met his death, was brought into evidence. Con-

cerning the admission of this evidence presented
by the defense, Mr. Snyder says:

"The court was composed of Hon. Hiram
Denio, presiding, who was one of the great
judges of the State, and Jonas Cleland, of War-
ren, John B. Dygert, of Frankfort, Abijah Os-
born, of Herkimer, and Richard Herrenden, of
Newport, were the side judges of the Common
Pleas. When the defense was reached, one of
the witnesses was asked, 'Did you ever hear this
Indian threaten to kill Foster?' To this the
District Attorney objected. Judge Denio held
the testimony to be inadmissable, when much
to his surprise and astonishment three of the
side judges announced that it was admissible,
thereby overruling Judge Denio's law. Under
this ruling of the side judges, Foster was permitted to prove that the Indian had threatened
to kill him. It is interesting to note that the
Court of Appeals subsequently in the Fisk-
Stokes murder case, substantially affirmed the
law promulgated by these side judges."

The summing up of Foster's attorney, Mr. E.
P. Hurlbut, is said to have been a masterly effort, full of pathos and tender references to the
aged prisoner at the bar. Many were moved to
tears by his eloquence.

In his charge the Court advised the jury that

"the law applied to the region of the country where the offense was committed. In regard to the race to which Peter Waters, the person named in the indictment, belonged," he said, "no one could take the life of such a one without such reasons as would authorize the taking the life of any other human being." His charge rather argued for conviction in some degree of murder or manslaughter. The jury retired and after a short deliberation returned. As the jurymen entered and took their seats, the crowded court room became hushed.

The moment, even more than is usual on such occasions, was one of intense interest. To so great a tension had the feelings of the old hunter been drawn by the excitement of the trial, that he now seemed hovering between life and death, and was insensible during the interrogation of the jury.

"Gentlemen of the jury," said the clerk, "have you arrived at a verdict?"

"We have," answered the foreman, "we find the prisoner not guilty."

A murmur of applause ran through the crowded chambers, but Foster was unconscious of it all. It was with considerable difficulty that he was roused to consciousness, so as to understand his fate. When the words "Not Guilty"

19

had been repeated to him several times, he appeared to realize their meaning, and rising up, he siezed Mr. Hurlbut, his chief counsel, with a grip which the Judge used afterward to say was "more than powerful," and straining him to his breast, exclaimed, "God bless you," then releasing his hold, he turned, and he stretched out both hands wide over the heads of the people that filled the court room, and exclaimed "God bless you all, God bless the people." His friends who were jubilant over the verdict then seized him, and placing him on their shoulders, marched in triumph through the streets of the village. Mr. Hurlbut and Foster never met again; as the old trapper soon after left the state. Mr. Hurlbut's fee for conducting the defense was fifty dollars, which Foster left with his son Amos, to give to his attorney. It was considered liberal compensation for those days.

The closing years of Foster's life were as peaceful and uneventful, as they well deserved to be. He had sold his farm at Salisbury to his son Amos in the summer preceding his trial. After his trial he spent sometime with his married children, after which he went with his wife to Wilkesbarre, Pennsylvania, where some of his relations lived. Simms says that he was afraid to remain in the country after killing the Indian at Old Forge. But this is highly improbable, as he had shot too many Indians in his days to be afraid of any of Drid's friends wreaking vengeance on him. It is true that he visited Fulton Chain but a few times after he shot Drid, but this was merely precautionary. He spent most of his time before going to Pennsylvania with his daughter Jemima, in the town of Ava, which was then on the very edge of Brown's Tract, and never displayed any fear of being molested.

Even in his new home in Pennsylvania, he continued to hunt a little. In his seventy-third year he shot a small deer about a mile and a half from his home. As of yore, he threw the carcass across his shoulders and started for home, but as he was ascending a hill a quarter of a mile from his house, he was taken with a severe pain in his chest, and distinctly felt something "give way," as he expressed it, in the region of his lungs. He struggled home, and fell fainting on the door steps, bleeding from the mouth. He rallied in a few days, and realizing that he could not live long, declared he must go to his daughter Jemima to die. Accordingly, as soon as he was able, he and his wife started on the long journey. They journeyed by

water as far as Rome, N. Y., where they procured a horse and driver, who took them to
Ava, a distance of fourteen miles. They
arrived at the home of his son-in-law David
Edgerton, the husband of Jemima, considerably
after dark; and wishing to have some fun with
his children, the old man sent the driver into
the house with instructions to ask "for lodging
for two old people who had made a long journey
that day, and could go no farther." After some
demurs, Mr. and Mrs. Edgerton finally said,
that if it would be any accommodation to the
aged travelers, they would take them in, but
still they said they did not see any reason why
they should not go on to the tavern. The driver
urged them, however, and they finally gave a
decisive and affirmative answer, when he withdrew and brought in Mrs. Edgerton's parents.
Great was their rejoicing, and the rejoicing of
their children, with whom they were great
favorites, especially grandpa, because of the
stories he used to tell them before he went away.

The old hunter lived less than a year after his
return to Ava. On the 14th of March, in 1840,
a sudden change came over him, which even his
young grand-children were able to detect, by
his changed demeanor; the absence of his cheery
words, and kindly attentions. His iron consti-

tution had worn out, and the mechanism of his
being was now propelled only by the momentum
given to it by its years of ceaseless activity.
Preparations were quickly made for his tender
care, by the loving ones who surrounded him.
A bed was prepared for him in the living room
of the house, while the members of the household vied with each other in their efforts to
make everything quiet and comfortable for
"grandpa."

The end came speedily. On the morning of
the 16th they saw it was approaching. Neighbors and friends gathered in kind solicitude.
His faithful wife sat by his bedside; his daughter
Jemima by the fireplace, with her youngest child,
a boy of three years, on her knees. The little
fellow slipped from his mother's knee, and approached the bed on which the dying hunter
lay; he stopped in the middle of the room, when
some one picked him up and carried him to the
bedside, that he might see his grandfather once
more. The old hunter recognized the child,
and his eyes lit up with a gleam of pleasure, and
he was gone.

And so he passed away; with the March wind
howling without, but with the cheerful singing
of a kettle hanging from a crane over the fire
within, his loving friends and family breathing

prayers for him, his own face illumed with a smile of peace. In the midst of such peaceful and hallowed surroundings, the old hunter and trapper went to meet his God.

Thus do we leave him, the hero of so many and gallant exploits. A hero, not because he killed a few Indians, whose rights have always been trampled upon; but a hero because of the sturdy character he developed and displayed in maintaining his own rights, as he saw and understood them; fearing, as his father had taught him, not the face of clay, but only the face of him in whose hands we leave him, who set his mark on the murderer Cain, and who extended mercy to Moses who slew a man, and concealed the body in the sands of the Egyptian plain.

9 783337 180393